THE LOVE SONG OF
j. edgar ho●ver

CHARLES TALKOFF

8th House Publishing
Montreal, Canada

Cover Art & Design © 2012 Jennifer Lamb

Title Font *Bleeding Cowboys* © Guillaume Seguin

Set in *Caslon Pro, Rough Typewriter* & *Century Gothic*

A CIP catalogue record for this book is available from

LIBRARY AND ARCHIVES CANADA

CATALOGUING IN PUBLICATION

The Love Song of J. Edgar Hoover/Talkoff, Charles (1965-)

ISBN 978-1-926716-10-7

8th House Publishing
Montreal, Canada

The Love Song of J. Edgar Hoover is Charles Talkoff's pick-up line to the hostesses of the Big House, the Canon, the Library, the Archive. In a dark, repressed corner in his heart of hearts there smolders, like the end of Castro's cigar, a burning desire to be embraced by Them and their minions. Yet Talkoff knows what happens to writers who become Company Men, Good Soldiers, and Government Agents. Talkoff's novel is full of such writers' struggles (and ultimate failures) to remain true to their art as well as free to pursue it. Talkoff himself has gone rogue. There is anthrax in this love letter to the creative Establishment and that pharmakon is paranoia. Like Hoover, Talkoff sucks information and informants dry, taps into conversations and communications, reads through other's correspondence and minds, spies on his neighbors, envisions connections and ghosts, and sniffs the panties of the Muse. One of the many lessons Talkoff teaches us in his first novel is that all great writers and artists act on such obsessive impulses.

For some, *The Love Song of J. Edgar Hoover* will seem the ramblings of a madman, although a well-read one. Where is the structure to make music out of this static? Where is plot, narrative? Where is this story going? Why won't it end? The same was said of the writing of William Burroughs, who appears and disappears throughout Talkoff's novel as is fitting for a writer nicknamed "el hombre invisible." Like with Naked Lunch, there is something obscene and criminal about Talkoff not making perfect sense, of not speaking clearly, of not making his intentions known.

Pardon me if I see Talkoff as a serial killer having his way with the entire body of literature, art, and popular culture. In "The Love Song of J. Alfred Prufrock," Eliot writes, "There will be a time to murder and create/And time for all the works and days of hands/That lift and drop a question on your plate." He is a master of collage, montage, and assemblage that is for certain. His modus operandi is cutting, dissecting, piercing, skewering, dismembering as well as pasting, linking, attaching, assembling, remembering. Talkoff's novel is after all "held together by crazy glue." The butchered corpus of Literature stitched to animate a Frankenstein's Bride. Or maybe I should say a Bride Stripped Bare By Her Bachelors, Even. That classic work of physics and desire. Or maybe the nude corpse in Duchamp's "Étant Donnés". The Black Dahlia as muse. On his darker side, sex, death, and conspiracy feed Talkoff's imagination.

For those who need something to grasp onto during Talkoff's wild ride, there is always the physics of Katzenberg's Super Atomic Piston Ring, a "machine that would allow the user to tap into conversations anywhere in the world at any moment in time." A reader could clutch tightly onto that Ring in the hopes of finding some fidelity to a story line, but I advise one to hang on loosely or else the Ring will self-destruct, like one of Jean Tinguely's metamechanics. Talkoff's novel is full of invisible men, like Chandler's chauffeur, who slip beyond the control of authorial intention. But on one level, the Ring can be viewed as the creative imagination, a flux capacitor that allows the author to move through time and memory. Or to turn the coin: the commercialization and commoditization of that imagination.

In the Ring, I see a reference to Jeffrey Katzenberg, CEO of DreamWorks Animation and former chairman of Walt Disney Company? For Talkoff, anything is possible. Everything is permitted and connected. Paranoia again. And to paraphrase Burroughs, sometimes paranoia is just having the facts.

The Ring, like *The Love Song of J. Edgar Hoover* itself, is a merely a deus ex machina enabling Talkoff to take flight and get on with the pleasure of processing his impressions on popular culture, art, literature, his sexual relationships, and his relationship with a world out to fuck him over. Feel free to mis-read Talkoff's novel. He will not mind; in fact he would love it. As Duchamp stated, "I believe that the artist doesn't know what he does. I attach even more importance to the spectator than to the artist."

In weak moments while reading the darker, more desperate passages of Talkoff's book, I wonder if I'll ever receive from him a packet of manuscripts and computer disks with the handwritten note, "Gone to Ketchum." Yet the obvious pleasure that Talkoff experienced in creating his novel dispels such thoughts. *The Love Song of J. Edgar Hoover* is not a swan song; it is ultimately an intelligent man's attempt to create a space for reading, writing, and thinking; a place in which to listen to the voices in his head, to converse with the voices of Literature, History and Art, and to escape the voice of popular opinion and establishment doublespeak. Talkoff does not ask for much: a room of one's own and some time to enjoy it. Unfortunately in today's world, that may be asking for far too much. I sincerely hope that this first novel published by 8th House opens for Talkoff the door to that room and grants him the time to settle in and explore it. Talkoff knows his literary history, so he is well aware that the small press has provided such keys to others before him. I think *The Love Song of J. Edgar Hoover* proves him worthy of such a gift.

-Jed Birmingham, *Author, Editor*

For D.S.

THE LOVE SONG OF J. EDGAR HOOVER

CHARLES TALKOFF

"In a closed society where everybody's guilty, the only crime is getting caught. In a world of thieves, the only final sin is stupidity."
— Hunter S. Thompson

Overture

Come metropolis soldiers where I am spread against the sky like a prisoner in your slinky cuffs of discipline. Let us go see hummingbird moths buzz making twilight a live wire of interrogation... Oh, do not ask, what does he mean; what does it mean...in the secret womb, the special agents come and the addicted informants go, saying: I'm held together by crazy glue, aren't you...?

Come metropolis soldiers, another date with that cliché history; with larval shadows and ideas, unmade... in the secret womb, the special agents come and go, saying: I'm held together by crazy glue, aren't you...?

In a roach-heavy hotel I passed my memory and broke myself as a plate in a sink and began to dare to eat my mind as a ripening peach... Oh, they shall say—whisper-whisper—there he goes, Ulysses *pretending* to be a drag queen (again: just another hash-baby who doesn't want to lay siege to Troy). Oh, do not ask, what does he mean; what does it mean... in the secret womb the special agents come, and go, saying: I'm held together by crazy glue, how 'bout you...?

Now, a ragged informant looking for a gossip fix buzzes in my vein—if we squeeze the ghost of J. Edgar Hoover like an accordion, will he cum spraying spy-spittle-seed, or will he wheeze and rise like a torn blow-up doll....?

Special Agent: Explain the network!?!

"I am not Prince Hamlet... a bit obtuse; at times, indeed, almost ridiculous—Almost at times, the fool..."

And now, the telephone rings in Arabic and New York emerges bleeding from my eyes and I wish only to be quiet in a quiet place and there find an age of sleep.

So, history is a dim rusty shovel and god digs and digs and we are the soil, and we are the earth and how I love you is every precious word, so come metropolis soldiers, let us go and spread ourselves across the night, as lovers do.

ॐॐ

The Fool

After the big rain made channels in the dirt, the earth was a map around a field of damp stones that were enormous breasts. The persistence of memory made my expedition arduous. Pine cones, a nickel, a bus pass, a blue button still trailing the umbilical string torn screaming from a shirt, a jacket; who can say? This is my crew. We were exhausted. Far away a great beast washed up on the shore. I sent the pinecone to make a reconnaissance. We waited patiently fearful that our presence would be detected before he returned.

All clear, he reported, wetly. It's a piece of the universe, disguised as driftwood.

I was unconvinced. The whole earth (do you hear what I'm telling you? I said: The whole earth) tilted just a little and between the very white sea spray and the very gray sky, we marked in our time upon our invisible map, the outermost edge of our time.

☒☒

Late at night, I harvest my skull using ideas as shovels. I work this field deep. There are rusty shoes, fur, books, paintings and photographs; beautiful pieces of charcoal and clean sheets of white paper, the past, women who open and close and open again the future arriving as a very blue bird stepping delicately between the tall reeds and blue moss electrified and sometimes, there is a sign. It says: *Touch me*.

So poems as loose change precisely planted

between the cushions of many chairs and couches...
and on the street, below the happy fog, even then
in late hours such as everyone knows, the earth
vibrates as an idea or a blueprint for constructing a
life or a cat and quietly before the mercy of sleep,
I remember that I've forgotten how using us as a
plough, god seeds the earth with blood and words.

༄༅

The Priestess

She is the girl who arrives bouncing like the night
except when she is the night who arrives bouncing
like a girl. She is very white, except when she is very
dark. Sometimes I know she comes from an island
where they cover themselves in the peat, and the
bogs stir silently in memory and loudly in gestures
encoded by ten thousand years of earth dirt. She
has every name.

Sometimes she comes from the desert. Her father
was a giant oak tree and sometimes he was a
mountain. It's often very confusing and often there is
a ram or a hero, a sacrifice and great rhythms chime
the hour.

When she is from the mythical land they call
Ireland, then her father is a singing fish in a leaky tub
or a tree with many branches and deep dark roots

that hold the earth like flesh; and when she is from the desert, her father is a bull or a star, a serpent or a spring, and you can think it's a metaphor as much as you like but I am telling you the truth, as clearly, cleanly and precisely as I know how.

When she is from the desert, she is dark and I see her naked in a side pool of a fast river and the river says, 'Oh, we are so much touching each other,' and her eyes are very very dark and she is ten thousand years old because DNA is a poem, an epic and a river that says oh hubbly-bubbly and oh.

When she is white-skinned and her eyes are gray and graygreen and bluegray and bluegreen and bluegraygreen as the sea or the day, she carries a dead god on a stick of wood.

She hangs it from her neck until it drags her down so far that she becomes an expert on the tops of people's shoes. And if you think this is pleasantly clever or amusing and charming somehow then you know nothing about girls and their fathers, fathers and their girls and your turtle mind is slow and forever as a turtle but soon enough you will learn and be turned on your back to die slowly in the sun.

They hang the dead god on a stick on many walls in their homes and they pretend to eat his flesh and drink his blood and count the days and the hours, and no one except the ones who finally snap like dry rubber-bands ever say, 'I feel flowers growing in my eyes,' and none but those who say nothing (and plan meticulously their escape, by tunnel, glider and underground rail), ever say anything at all but have a pious silence because they know silence is holy.

✄ ✄

The Fool, the Priestess & the King of Swords

So, she does not carry that anymore but still, because we are so small and the great king has made a terrible war in far far Babylon and the mad prophet has come again screaming out of the desert, we shiver in the day as if the day were naked and ashamed and had the certain knowledge of death and to ward off the evil, we have a clock in the shape of a cat and the cat's tail swishes the hours and the cat's eyes move side to side.

The cat makes us smile and our cats are both black and one is bigger than the other and the big one likes to sit on books and to chew plastic—but don't ask me why—and the other one we found in the park likes to sleep under blankets or on your lap and this is one component for the secret formula to Katzenberg's Super Atomic Piston Ring that *The Ministry of Ambiance* searches for but can never find because it is right in front of them and they are very dry in stern hours and they are bad actors demanding answers to questions no one has asked, scurrying and secretly hiring people to be snitchy informants twitching for a gossip-fix that never satisfies and they listen and listen and pour over transcripts and intercepts and often say: Ah-ha!

But then, the trees snore loudly at them and terrible things go on happening and good things too and *The Ministry of Ambiance* has many deep tunnels and the files grow in sealed rooms like the biggest cities with small electric cars and mechanical arms and traffic lights and street signs and there, no one is ever happy.

⌀⌀

The Observer & the Observed

A beautiful woman comes into a café. She is Russian and looks like a ballerina in a movie about a Russian ballerina and her face is glacial, regal, and sometimes she sits on a terrace in Vienna and it is 1913 and everyone is frozen, then moves very slowly, and Thomas Mann is watching them and he is very serious. He feels a wrinkle in time and the wave washes over him and he writes down the code for recognizing the way the waiters move as the dots and dashes signaling cataclysm. He drinks a lot of coffee and watches everything with great big tiger eyes and I am watching the Russian woman who is aloof, regal, beautiful and smells of new money with brain enough to make it look old. She sits in the café and waits. A young girl who resembles her and an old woman who looks as she will look later when she appears again in another story come into the café and they sit together speaking Russian while outside it rains because the Russians (like everyone else) have stories with rain and snow and long long long remembrances and now the Russians are us, and we are them entwined strands of a story called DNA in G-sharp and F and A and so on, etc, etc, and the little girl touches the fur trim on the beautiful woman's right sleeve and the beautiful woman jerks her arm away to fix her hair which does not need fixing or anything except a stroke from a hand softly and soon she leaves as if for an appointment and you know she is being paid for it and everything suddenly constricts, freeze-dried and zip-locked for storage with a label that reads: *Just Add Writer.*

✍ ✎

The Lovers, Part I

I'm cruising down Nelly Street with the very beautiful white-skinned girl. She's got a spear, and a necklace made from bones. You can't see them, but I can.

When the Romans come, she'll kill many of them and there will be a great feast and a lot of brutal greasy titanic ritualized sex and the severed heads of the Romans will hang before tents and there will be grunting in the dark because time goes in every direction at once.

In the meantime, we go to a health food store where the neo-Amazonian Ukrainian girl beeps and flashes and whirls like a disco queen whose throne is made of roller skates. Soon-to-be-faded and dilapidated like-a-palace-after-the-revolution, intellectual Russian boys flock around her trying to dock with her breasts but so far they have no luck, and you can see them brooding in cafés in Little Odessa hunched over their siege equipment drawing diagrams, making models to scale with the angle of her magnificent breasts relative to the slope of their rampant cocks and their eyes are very hungry.

So, in the health food store we go shopping and we talk to Troy. He's a film maker and tells funny stories and has a kind wit that he shares sometimes shyly and sometimes with tender irony, but mostly he is from Vermont and pours slowly.

Later we buy some smoke from Mister Jellybean and he's a lutheran-buddhist-agnostic who says: I accept Jesus Christ as my savior and he introduces us to his wife who is from Mother India and was raised by evangelical Baptists.

She points to a doll on their bed and says in a voice that scares you half to death, 'I have a baby too,' and she is a child of children, tyrannical fierce and narrow, who are each a dull shopping mall where every store sells the same thing and at night metal curtains come down and the merchandise is put away in pleasing rows and after smoking we have sex sweaty and languid and find in each other every trauma, hurt, wound, ache and desire and we bruise each other terribly and we realize Mr. Jellybean is a snitch for the *Ministry of Ambiance* so we let him go spiraling down into the black hole of history and silence and these are the times we live in and who can say anything about it except these sweet rags of growing young again.

ᢒᢐ

A King of Broken Cups

So, the pretty, very white-skinned girl's father was an oak tree and he lived in Minnesota and was raped by a priest repeatedly, and that's an old story full of blood excrement and humiliation and the turning of sex inside out emerging as the shaking desire to receive communion holy true and electric.

There were rules and accidents that were never accidents and the rules were changed to suit the circumstances of broken desire, so of course the oak tree that was her father had sex with the broken glass that was her mother and she was pregnant and they married and he went door to door selling meat in the early days of *Dubliners* and Jim Joyce said: 'You shall know him by these signs,' and I did and he drove a big American car from the fifties, smoked cheap cigars and his little blue eyes were sad, mean and fearful, and he called grown men lad, (if they were waiters or attending him somehow), ate his meals quickly without joy as joy, but anxiety as pleasure and then he had a heart attack and was erased from existence in that form and was recycled and became someone else with encoded memories that popped open like dark wet flowers or doors expanding in the heat.

The Deceivers

In the heat the room like shrink-wrap constricts thinking and thinking expands to include, enclose this idea: The fat woman who lives across the street harnesses flesh and Audrey who is the very white skinned girl says she remembers living in Paris and knowing Gargantuan Jean who would never allow anyone to see him sit down, or stand up—no, he would say, it is inconceivable (she said, knowing-remembering to convey wistfulness as sex; as if to say, I know-remembering and will hold you with it between my legs by saying this is my knowledge of life) and the fat woman makes me remember Audrey and her way of speaking with a southern accent when she wants to play at being a Tennessee Williams or William Faulkner wild drunk slut who begs to be fucked up the ass while screaming, *oh, Daddy,* or shoot empty gin bottles with a .22 pistol she calls *Brick,* and the first morning after the first night she said I dreamed you were sitting in a chair next to my father in a chair and his chair was much bigger than yours and she had the good grace to laugh mostly at her own self and to only cut me a little with her vapor-knife and honest the hours walk till they wobble and break down as perfect equations for building a life or a shoe.

☙❧

Shadow of the Fool & the Lovers, Part II

Good Christ, but it's hot. I mean the walls, without insulation, exposed all day to the sun, get so warm that the tape I'm using to hold my drawings peels, melts, drips sticky adhesive like semi-dried cum, and the drawings slide and I think of Jorge Picardo who paints so badly but sculpts well enough and lives here in our new bohemia; this true *Montmartre* where the artists live only because it's cheap but never cheap enough and the noise never stops and Jorge is another drunk almost always ready to spring like a jack rabbit of violence hopping, punching the air in the dead run of violence that comes from the Spain of his memory and lands in the San Francisco of his life and when he says as an artist you should come to an *Alcoholics Anonymous* meeting, I know and Audrey knows he's asking for company because he says he had god when he was in Spain and he doesn't want to substitute booze for god and he wages an endless trench war in his mind going over the top, slaughtering himself and rising again and the bottle blows the charge but he's lost weight and sleeps better and doesn't spend his time with the other drunks who never want anything good he says (and his paintings are some combined horde from the burial mounds of a disco as if mile-high boots and mood rings and gold leaf on red paint were all Tut or the bust of Nefertiti or even a long ship pulled from the bogs of Scandinavia) and Audrey says she's worried that if Jorge sees my paintings or reads what I'm writing he'll start drinking again; that he may hit me and he's not especially large but he's built like a short brick wall with legs and then there's still

14

the drinking and the hysterical Latin-thing patented three hundred years ago by *El Greco* and refined for world-wide distribution by *Goya* and the Jesuits in which content is subordinate to expression and drama is the point—Well, hell, I say, leaning a little closer to the telephone so that *The Ministry* can hear me all the better—imagine a man exploding like the fourth of July—all those memories of lace mantillas and wax figures under glass and the heat and the cool dead spaces of big churches with leprous blood soaking the stale air that walks centuries at a time from the treasure ships of conquest to Pablo fucking Maya and thinking of Françoise who took it like Olga who became Fernande (or the other way around) and the nose next to the strange eye in the painting that looks like Greco but isn't and from one lane of thought to the next with no speed limit except those imposed by something called rules, or *The Ministry*, Audrey, bent over the table in the sort-of-kitchen of our too-tiny overpriced apartment is moaning and letting out, 'Oh daddy more, I need it more I've been so naughty do you see me, tell me you're watching me daddy' and I say knowing *The Ministry* is recording everything that sexing them is the thing and that's a play and Audrey coming is a wonder because she gets a little quiet and a cry comes up deep from within and she shakes and shivers, cries a whimper and splash of pleasure and her hips flare

15

out curving 'round and down and I've got my fingers dug into her ass and she's bucking and we're riding it until she arches her back, her head swings side to side and then she goes and comes back slowly as a hand opening after touch has departed like some sort of approximation of the end of the world screaming 'Daddy! Daddy! Daddy!' and falls over in a growling exhausted electrically charged pile of skin and desire as a small wave pulls back from the shore and the sand is left glassy smooth like paint that never dries.

☙❧

King, Queen, Pnin

And then the very next time I see Jorge he's strung out twitchy the way informants get terrified of being sent down and away and I feel badly for him until he starts asking me about Audrey and then he goes on about this girl he wants and he says yeah I'm going to bend her over in my kitchen and fuck her until she screams *ay papi!*

He says it with a sharp snap of his tongue busting out each word with a thrust and his eyes get big waiting for my reaction. I just look away and stare at the photographs on the walls. We're in a café, a generic nowhere place on the Boulevard in Little

Odessa and he's so nervous he can't keep still and one minute he's jitter-bugging his legs under the table and the next he's working a double espresso to his mouth like coffee is about to be outlawed and he's watching the door and watching me and he asks what I think about the girl and bending her over in the kitchen and I say it all sounds like Orwell meets Nabokov.

—Nabokov?

—Yeah, my pal Sebastian knows him.

—You mean the old guy runs the Russian deli over on 18th?

—Sure.

He stares at me; mute, confused and full of fear that leaks from his eyes in a steady invisible stream.

—How's the novel going? he says

—Great.

—What's it about?

He's still bouncing his legs and then he starts spooning sugar into his coffee.

—Mistaken identities. Paranoia. Rounding up the usual suspects.

—What's that mean? You mean like that movie with the guy who fakes being a gimp?

—Like Rosencrantz and Guildenstern delivering their own letters of transit.

He stares at me uncomprehending, momentarily mute, his fingers tapping the sides of his coffee cup.

—I don't understand, he says, what does that mean?

—Those fellows are not friends of the king.

—Does it make a pattern?

—Sure.

—Can you explain it?

—You could count yourself the king of infinite space.

—But?

—But, I said and stood up; if you listen to everyone's conversation, then everything becomes suspect and no one can say anything anymore.

He looked sad all of a sudden sad the way you get when your dog dies and you know it's never coming back and the victory I had over him is there for a second because it only means I'm immune to him but irrevocably alone and the air is a rope constricting all of us and the air is a great eye that never blinks and is watching everyone.

✄ ✃

The Cards Reverse

Yffat kisses Audrey for one million, nine-hundred and fifty-three reasons, and because Yffat can't be a man and her father wishes she were a man but she's not and she keeps trying but it never works, she insists she's going to make a movie where the lesbians are all beautiful (subjective concepts of objective criteria duly noted) and none of them have hairy chins because she's sick of it and she likes them white and blonde like Audrey but she's in lust with Golfidin who is dark (because eight hundred years ago, Godfrey of Lyon raped a girl so Gol has plasma-green eyes that make Yffat forget what day it is) and she wants her precisely because she's Tunisian and Arab and it excites her and so she kisses Audrey and they make love until lapping at Audrey's pussy, Yffat brings her out moaning *no, no, no* and the whole universe quivers.

The Magus

In the country of the novel there is a junta that rules everything. In the country of the novel there is a general with the head of a rabbit who rules the junta. In the mind of the general there is order. Within that order there is a library of everyone in the world. Every day the general draws a new line on his map of heaven.

I am reading the novel and I am reading about the man from the *Ministry* who speaks to the general. In the evening, when the cool winds blow across the harbor and the leaves of the banana trees drift back and forth the general likes to sit on the balcony of his palace and sip mint tea.

The man from the *Ministry* whispers in one of the generals fluffy ears.

—Take all the men and bring them to the highest mountain, El Corazon, and throw them into the sea.

—Well, says the general, holding his tea cup and saucer above his lap. If we do as you say, my friend, and we take all the men and throw them from the highest cliff into the sea, who; who my friend, will utilize the women?

The man from the ministry scratches his chin with his right hand, and places his left upon the arm of the general's chair. He leans close and again whispers in the general's fluffy ear.

—We will provide advisors.

—As you say, says the general, sipping his tea; as you say.

In the country of the novel the man who is supposed to be me closes the book and watches the author walk into the park. His name is Ariel. I am sitting on a bench and I watch him walk past a knot of *au pairs* with children and strollers. Pigeons move in feathery lines of gray along the narrow strip of sand at the edge of the water. Ducks drift along the surface of the water and through the clouds sunlight falls in small splashes making shadows on the lake.

—Well, hello old sport, says Ariel.

He comes at me, squarely, wide shoulders at a slight stoop, his big bush of black-grey hair flopping up and down, and he sits on the bench pulling a gold cigarette case from inside his jacket.

—So, how do you like the book?

—Just great. The story of the man who sold his shadow.

He opens the case and nods his head. It is a little after three and the *au pairs* are taking their children out for a last afternoon walk through the park. Across from us, beyond the lake they stand near the set of swings talking in loud Irish rhythms.

Old Russian men sit on benches by the water reading and watching the ducks. The men have made hats from newspapers and are wearing them on their heads.

Ariel lights a cigarette with a lighter and takes in a long deep lung-filling blast, then exhales a thick stream of blue-grey smoke that curls inside itself and extends out into the air and fades.

—It is funny, he says, putting the lighter and cigarettes back into his jacket where they live; the way things agreed.

It wasn't really a question so much as a statement disguised as a question and I said nothing. He worked on his cigarette and the light moved on the water.

—When I lived in Xanadu, he said, I had no sense of the world beyond my street. I lived above my father's store and that was the farthest reach of the world as far as I knew. Men would come to the store and my brothers and I and my sisters, we all existed like bees humming there and the things we sold were honey from the hive and that was the world.

He examined the cigarette. The tip faintly red, extended as the paper burned away back towards his thick fingers. A thin wave of smoke rose upwards describing a curving line that settled into a small cloud above us.

—Men would come and my father served them tea in glasses. He had an ornate samovar. He cleaned it every day. The men would drink tea and play backgammon and talk. They called it conversation but it was really gossip distilled and then hyper-distilled. Of course for me everything changed when I went to university.

He paused, for effect, and examined the tip of his cigarette, and then took another extravagant drag. He blew three smoke rings and smiled.

—You never should have dropped out, he said. There was such potential for you. And this clichéd dialogue; the scene it's all so banal. You really should have understood that.

—I had other things I wanted to do.

—Other things, he said, *really*. If it were to be at all something you could prove, it would be false, which contradicts the premise and the idea that in any consistent system, provable statements are always true.

—Said the Hatter to the teapot.

I shrugged my shoulders. The light moved across the water and the ducks drifted in and out of the shadows. The breeze sifted the leaves of the trees and the trees shook sounding like water running full and fast from a faucet.

—And you know, he said, I am doing you a favor.

—How's that?

He took a last pull on his cigarette and flicked the dead end out towards the gravel in front of the bench. I watched it turn end over end and land on the ground.

—I told them it was useless for me to wear a wire; you'd never fall for it. And even if you did, you'd see what I was doing and start one of your insufferable monologues full of irritating and cryptic references to your obscure heroes.

He stopped and coughed. He spit a long phlegm-rich wad out of his mouth. It flew thickly and landed with a snap, stitching itself wetly into the ground, reflecting a snot-green patina.

—I don't have heroes. And obscurity is not what it seems.

—Oh holy cool one you are so sublime. Perhaps a little Vortex Sutra to show everyone how hip you are.

—What do you want?

He turned and smiled at a woman who jogged passed us. Then he reached into his jacket and pulled out the case and the lighter. He went through the ritual again. A child detached from the knot of *au pairs* and ran down towards the water. The pigeons rose in a gray column, turned, and filled the air over the lake like a mass of small crosses, then landed where they had been.

—They want to know how you can see them. They believe you understand Katzenberg. They want you to explain the system; how can you see them how do you know what they know?

I watched the ducks drifting over the water. I ran my hands over the book. I looked at the cover.

—Everything makes a pattern, I said.

—Explain it to them.

—No.

—It's idiocy, he said, and laughed a long thick cloud of smoke. His eyes were big and black. His hands were big and hair curled thickly over his knuckles.

—We'll get out.

—Oh, Christ, he said, how fucking quixotic of you; you and the fractured muse; it's like trying to date Leda after the rape. Tell me where are you going to go?

I watched a woman with brutally short hair scoop up the child who had raced after the birds. The ducks turned as a fleet and paddled into the center of the lake.

—Away from here, I said.

—Oh, he said, where is that on the map?

—What do you want?

—I told you, they want to know how you can see them. They invest a lot of time in being invisible; time and effort. They think you're a professional. Or a sport of nature. And they are curious. They are going to find the truth about Katzenberg and they think you know. They will pay you. They will pay you a lot. You can have everything. They will give you whatever you want.

—They never fit the pattern. And that generates another pattern which is anomalous. And they're just really bad actors. If you can't tell the spooks from everyone else you're blind.

—Explain it to them.

—This is pointless. *Non Servitor*. The secret is in the trees.

—For fuck's sake don't throw Joyce at me.

—Do you believe in anything?

—You know, he said, crossing one leg over the other, I saw a movie the other day, and it made me think of you.

—I'm thrilled.

—Yes, he said, sucking on his cigarette, this man tells a story, and the man listening says, 'that's a hell of a story,' and the first man, the man telling the story to the second man, says, 'no, that's not a hell of a story; I'll tell you a hell of a story,' and the second man looks curious and the first man, he says, 'Charlie Chaplin enters a Charlie Chaplin look-a-like contest, and comes in third. Now that's a story.'

He smiled wetly and inhaled the smoke burning up from the cigarette. The trees bent a little in the wind and the *au pairs* drifted further down the path into the park. A man with a newspaper hat stood and pulled a bag from his jacket. He walked to the edge of the water and began to throw pieces of bread to the birds. The ducks and the pigeons came to him and made a great surging mass of feathers.

—Perhaps you can steal that one for your next novel.

—If you didn't want them to record you, you should have kept your mouth shut.

—And just what do you think they will do with you?

He laughed. He coughed and when he was done he sucked on his cigarette and then coughed again. When he was done he looked at me.

—They will either kill you, he said, or you'll work for them, or, you will kill your self and save them the trouble of spending a bullet or throwing you off a roof.

His voice was flat but his eyes were big and his lips trembled. A great blue heron came in over the tree tops and glided down towards the tall reeds at the side of the lake. It pulled back its wings to brake and then extended its long wire legs. It was flying and then, all at once, it was stepping through the reeds, its long thin neck and tiny head moving back and forth like a feathered piston.

—We're getting out.

—She'll leave you first. It's always that way.

—You're ridiculous.

—My novels get reviewed. I travel. I contribute to newspapers, magazines; I lecture at the best universities. People give me things I have no use for. I've signed a movie deal, fucked models. I have more women than I know what do with. You, you're broke, depressed, and no one wants your work, and when you do manage to find a gallery or a publisher, look what happens; they follow your calls, your mail, and arrest everyone you speak with. And you waste away with the drunks and the frauds. And I'm ridiculous.

—We're getting out.

—There's nowhere to go. Go down any road, you'll find yourself in the same place. You live in a box. They've put you in a box. They watch you all the time. There's nowhere to go. They watch everyone. They listen to everyone. Privacy is dead and on display in a museum somewhere right next to the caveman and the Dodo. And if you resist you will be burned at the cyber-stake. Live on pay-per-view. Coover wasn't a complete idiot you know.

—You do not exist.

—Oh, how metaphysical of you; what's next, no man is an island? Perhaps a little O'Hara for some jazzy interludes between bouts of enhanced interrogation?

—They own you.

—They own everyone. Empire Incorporated. Murder Incorporated. It's the greatest snuff film in history and you have a role.

—Go fuck yourself.

He laughed. He finished his cigarette. He dropped it on the ground. He looked at it and then he reached into his jacket and pulled out a small box. In the box was a jump drive.

—This is for you.

—What is it?

—A story, he said, a fable.

—I don't want it.

—It's the fable of Audrey and Yffat, he said, and laughed. The narration is outstanding. All very post-mod meta-fiction with a touch of multi-culturalism and taboo-lit. It's really quite sublime.

He stood and looked across the water.

—Ducks, he said, by god, ducks.

He looked at me, and smiled.

—Everyone is a spy, he said. Everyone is a spy in

their own life and a spy in the lives of others. It's all so very East German. Like a glimpse into chaos.

—Go to hell.

—Oh blank confusion, he said. No law, no meaning and no end.

—You can make as many references as you like but you're still a whore.

—Be seeing you, he said.

He walked down the gravel path, his hands in his jacket pockets. I watched him go until he was out of the park. I looked at the birds. The ducks drifted on the water. Finches came and went in orderly gusts. The pigeons moved into the park pecking near the benches. The benches were empty except for one old man wearing a newspaper hat. He was watching the pigeons.

In the novel, within the country of itself, time passes. Later in the narrative, things happen that cannot be explained. Existence is sequential but non-linear. In the winter, there is rain. Sometimes, it snows.

The narrator, who is supposed to be me, listens to Coltrane turn Greensleaves inside out, upside down and backwards yet true and going and sentences of music start in the middle and reach for their predicate and subject at the same time, time being elastic, speeding up, slowing down, turning, a circle and a wedge and waves of water form on the surface of the water and jagged light and coffee hands make hungry ideas flap their wings. Tinfoil heart reflects love, warps easily, and rough crevasses encode memory because the savage god is its own piston.

Long after these events, when Audrey had fled, or been taken, or perhaps both, when the narrator had been taken by god to another place in the story, he wrote about coffee hands and how hungry ideas flap their wings. And everyone was being watched and everyone was being listened to and later people would say, 'but how did it happen how did it happen that they were all being spied upon and how was it that everyone began to sound the same and use the same words?' and no one would answer them because everyone already knew the truth; they were all collaborators and everyone was afraid. Then, a new character appeared. We will call her Samantha. Perhaps that is her true name. He tells her about flapping ideas and his tinfoil heart.

—I don't understand, says Samantha. She is confused. She is angry. She is angry because she is confused because the story makes her feel stupid even though she is not stupid. She wants things to make sense.

—I don't understand, she says, how can you tell someone is an informant; how can you tell they work

30

for the Ministry? It makes no sense.

—They're obvious. Their voices always give them away. The secret in their eyes.

—If, she says, you ever do get something published, you'll be one of those guys who gets a ten-thousand dollar advance from some small press and no one will ever know you exist and no one will ever understand what you've written because it will not be like what they already know.

She places the pieces of paper on the table in the sudden no-man's land that has appeared between them. The plates on the table are moats, and the forks and knives are catapults, and the baggage trains for the siege that is their love, stretch for miles into childhoods dimly glimpsed.

※ ※

The surface of his love begins to look like the skin of a deflated balloon. He writes: My love looks like the skin of a deflated balloon and my skin begins to look like love deflated inside a dead balloon and the balloon begins to look like me; deflated and letting go of the string he drifts down the street weakly bouncing and colliding from pole to car to door, and everyone sees that he's inside out, and they ignore him or run as if he's contagious.

He writes all of this and what he writes is recorded

by the *Ministry of Ambiance* and within the within of the within of the within of the Ministry, Special Agent Automatic Turpentine reads the transcript and he counts the letters, the vowels and the consonants, searching for the secret to the code that will reveal the truth about the Super Atomic Piston Ring, but he finds only the words and he begins to weep.

He shakes and spasms vibrate through him and his tears fly from his face as elongated glimmering blue salmon. Special Agent Automatic Turpentine holds on to the corners of his office desk as if he were in the cockpit of a rocket.

☙ ❧

Samantha sits on the porch with her best gal-pal Darla, drinking wine. It is a lazy summer evening and the fireflies are blinking on and off in the deepening dark like advertisements for nature. The red neon sign that says: *BANK*, casts a shallow puddle on the sidewalk.

Darla says, what were you thinking and Samantha stares at her phone and says, I'm not going to call him, and the gathering evening heat. mixed within the dark mixed within itself, rolls in and out over the city and Darla's big orange cats watches the lights blinking in the air with steady hungry cat eyes.

℘ℚ

He, who is I and not, sits on the roof staring at the lights and shadows of Alexandria. The river fades in gathering twilight tremble, Lorca's ghost sings a song and flows slowly like a vast exposed vein of the earth. He remembers—: He says to Samantha—I am being watched. There is a tap on my phone. My mail is being read. I am being followed. They think I am someone I am not; they are making copies of me repeating what I say.

℘ℚ

Samantha sits on the porch drinking wine. Darla is in the kitchen getting a bottle of white from the refrigerator. The light within the fridge is morgue-white. It makes the bottle of wine look like a yellow cannon shell. Darla remembers trying to open and close the door of a fridge when she was very young, just fast enough to catch the light going on and off as if catching the moment of creation.

℘ℚ

He sends Samantha an email. He says: I wrote this. He writes about coffee hands and flapping wings and jagged light. He says, I lived on a Greek island and worked on a fishing boat; taught English. I met a man who came from far away. He was covered with exotic stamps and visas of memory and torture as if his body were a passport and language a border across which no one could trespass. He told me stories. He said ill fares the land. He said the earth is sick.

❦

A machine of great complexity records every stroke of every key on the keyboard. Special Agent Automatic Turpentine reads the transcript. He sends a secure memo. He is within the within of the vast machine. It hums and whirs and buzzes and it has many rooms. It listens to everything including itself. It listens to everything but understands nothing.

❦

Coffee hands flapping their wings. This is a code. This is a code. The code is a code reflecting the code that states the code of flapping coffee and hands going through the air as wings. Many men sit in a room and read the words. Special Agent Automatic Turpentine sits in another room and waits to be told what to do next.

ℬℚ

I, who am he, sits on a bench looking up at the building in which he who is I, lives in an apartment that looks over the city and across the city to the river. The building is gray. The building is a vast cement carbuncle squatting on a low hill. The building looks like something Stalin would have ordered from a catalogue.

He sees himself flying off the roof. The building is gray and death can be multicolored. He has a pair of wings but they seem to only work in one direction.

A car glides past him. The car turns in the parking lot. It stops. Two men get out of the car. They lean on the hood of the car. Small cork-screw wires emerge from the ear-pieces they wear. They are wearing mirrored sunglasses. They stare at him. He sees himself reflected in their glasses. He is elongated; thin. They stare at him. He stares at them. They stare at him staring at them. The coal train chuffs in the near distance working down the track as a muscle of history.

ℬℚ

Samantha stands in front of a Degas at the National Gallery. A table before a window and on the table, bottles and a bowl of fruit. This is the moment of their beginning as it first appears and later he writes with joy did tumble I, the day unfolding out of darkness, as any acrobat of love, and he writes until the Ministry wraps tightly a block upon the border of ideas but still the earth is a sentry everything passes.

By then Samantha was gone and sitting on the stoop, much further along within the narrative, watching the trees sway as a chorus singing the wind, he remembered her saying: I don't care about your story; this is a terrible time to live and you have to be clever and act as if they are not watching everyone and he listens to the train pulling into Camden Station and he knows the night is a passionate soul full of codes unbreakable and from within the vault, deeply concealed, distilled, hyper-distilled and refracted endlessly, Special Agent Automatic Turpentine flaps his hands in the stale underground air and watches coffee drip slowly from a filter, down deep into a large coffee pot, filling slowly with every idea.

☙☙

Surveillance

I go out of the house and a man walks slowly behind me stiffly moving his long legs. I stop at the corner and go to my left and he goes to his left. I turn and walk to my right and he turns and walks to his right and I stop and he stops and stares at the window of a car. Somewhere close at hand a video camera records everything. I walk down the street and he walks down the street. I go home and he walks to the other side of the street and stares at me as I close the door.

✄ ✎

Surveillance

Audrey and I are in a museum. The museum is showing prints from the Meiji. Elegant yet stiff figures stand in the attitude of imperial domination and submission. A man follows us around the museum. He circles around us; always steps so he is behind us so we turn and circle behind him and he steps again so he is behind us and then we get to the last room and I whisper to Audrey and we run.

We run down the hall and then stop, turning suddenly into an alcove and wait and then, seconds behind us, he comes running down the hall and stops at the exit. We step out and stand behind him and he turns, slowly, stares at us with a blank face then, walking backwards, he goes out into the parking lot and we watch as a plain rental car pulls up and he gets into the passenger side, and the car leaves.

❡❡

I vomit my fear into the toilet and the mess of everything there makes a pattern and from deep within everything there are echoes and things are not required to make sense and there is the slow nauseating presence of fear and strangers watch you walk past them and pull out their phones and say your friend just walked by and if you tell anyone that this is happening they say you're an insane strand of the insane and you're contagious and this is how the machine works the gears grinding and you lie in bed and listen to them listen to you breathe.

❡❡

I closed the book, and sat on the bench and watched the birds coming and going across the water of the lake.

❡❡

Tiresias Speaks

"Just the minute the FBI begins making recommendations on what should be done with its information, it becomes a Gestapo."

— J. Edgar Hoover

A Queen of Cups

Yffat talks about Paris. She talks about the *Palais du Sal*. She is from Jerusalem. She combs exploding busses from her hair. These are called fragments of memory like a cookie and a cup of tea and the cup is cracked and so are the memories and the memories cut like shrapnel. She laughs and does an excellent imitation of Joan of Arc. She bursts into flames and then extinguishes herself with a ripe mango.

—That's a hell of a trick, I say.

She laughs again. When she laughs the day pulls a blanket over its face and hides because her laughter is heartbreaking and the day does not want to cry.

—Is the ocean a metaphor, she asks, or a fact?

—Perhaps, it is both, or neither.

—Is a novel an argument, or a seduction?

—It is a formula for the grand unified theory of everything.

—Perhaps, she says, it is both, or neither.

—It is as if your hands were small dark birds that do not know their way home.

—Ariel should not be trusted under any circumstances, she says.

—Have you read the book?

She smiles and shakes her head. She is sitting on the couch leafing through a fashion magazine.

—I'll wait, she says, for the movie.

—What do you think?

—I think this reality is a vast Byzantine Ponzi-scheme in which the car you buy today becomes an explosive vest the following week. Cell phones and genocide and the boy in the song about the boy in the bubble.

We laugh together and watching her I see her look at a long curl of her long curling black hair.

—Oh, she says, look, it's Golda Mier. I had wondered where she had got herself to.

It is a fog-heavy day and the big bay window is gray and moist. Yffat has no land line and no computer. She keeps her cell phone in her freezer so no one can listen to her conversations.

Her blue cat sits on the edge of the couch watching birds flit back and forth across the window.

—Read me that chapter, she says.

She puts the magazine down and closes her eyes. Her hair spills down over the red pillow under her head. *Kind of Blue* is on the stereo. The cat swishes its tail. A street car goes by and the floor vibrates. Blue and green sparks shoot off of the wires above the street.

In the country of the novel, where the rabbit-headed general presides over the junta, the ageless Foreign Minister Hans Metternich says, 'Power is the ultimate aphrodisiac' and the men of the junta laugh, knowingly. They smoke cigars. They drink excellent scotch. They listen to recordings of people being tortured. The rabbit-headed general drinks mint tea. Alcohol does not agree with his delicate constitution.

Metternich says: Once the government has taken the decision, the people owe their obedience to the government. The men nod their heads. A Victrola plays Caruso. The record snaps and pops under the needle.

Then the shadow of history appears like a red wine stain on the white tablecloth sitting over the vast table in the dining room where the junta has been entertaining Herr Metternich. The stain spreads quickly. The stain continues to grow and soon it is dripping off the tablecloth to the floor.

Servants come and wipe the growing puddle with cloth but the puddle continues to grow. Herr Metternich looks at his shoes. They are quite red. His socks feel uncomfortably wet and sticky. He examines his pocket-watch.

—I really should be going, he says, but the room is awash in the stain, and pieces of ornate furniture begin to bob back and forth on the rising tide, blocking his exit.

☙❧

In the Country of the Novel

In the country of the novel there is a lawyer from Madrid. He is hunting war criminals. He is hunting the truth. He calls the author and the author picks up the phone to say – this telephone does not work.

In the country of the novel the author is a prisoner. Another man, another artist, spoke highly of him but the Ministry was listening and placed a tap on another phone and they found a means to blackmail him.

They said, we know that your mistress is spying on the Senator for the rebels. We know everything about her, about you, about when you eat and what and when you sleep. We know what you sound like in the bathroom. Work for us or we will have ten thousand men rape her.

So, he agrees and they feed him lines from what the other artist said and he wrote a story and in the country of the novel, the author shoots himself, but kills the wrong person.

It is a magic bullet, says the Senator. He is leading the investigation into the suicide that was a murder. It is in all the papers. There is a beautiful woman named Utta Pepe who is the mistress of the author and the senator. There are many photographs of her in the press.

People sit in bars and at home and watch people

on television discuss the suicide that was a murder and the murder that was a suicide. A magic bullet, they say, certainly that is proof of the existence of god.

People come from all over the world to stand before the grave of the murder-that-was-a-suicide. They ask for a cure to their blindness, their mangled legs and stunted arms. They pray for a cure to their halitosis for a cure to their mysterious moles that look like the faces of dead saints. Someone writes a song called, the ballad of the magic bullet, and it is made into a video which creates a dance craze which spreads across the planet. This is reflected in the country of the novel.

In the newspapers I read that the critics find this to be boring self-reflexive modernity run amok. On the next page after the review, there is another lengthy review of the war in Babylon and Audrey asks me what they say.

—They say they believe that Gilgamesh can be defeated. They only ask for more time to expand the surge and create stability.

—What do you say?

—I find that to be boring self-reflexive modernity, run amok.

—As you say, says Audrey, as you say.

∅ ত

The Lovers, Part III

Yffat says you can have old karma in a new form, or new karma in an old form. She is not optimistic. Her optimism sits in a coffee can she keeps in the freezer.

She is listening to Louis Armstrong and the Hot Fives and Hot Sevens. She is swaying her hips in the room with the couch and the big window. She says, it is almost certainly the end of the world. She says the plague is again returned to London and swiftly.

She says that when she was a student and lived in Xanadu she knew Ariel and he would come to the bookstore where she worked.

He came every Tuesday at twelve. They talked about books, music, artists. He seduced her. He said angels and devils waged unending war in the curls of her long black hair.

They did it in the bookstore, in the small back room. Books would fall to the floor and they would read them, believing they had opened randomly. On the other side of the door there was a narrow alleyway. At one end a blind man sold coins. He said each coin was a story. Ariel made up stories for each coin and whispered them into the ears of the angels and devils that waged unending war in the curls of her long black hair. At the other end of the alleyway a man who had taught physics in Leningrad played the violin. There were more out-of-work physicists in Xanadu than anywhere in the world. He played Russian folk tunes and sold books that contained the formulas for describing the curvatures of quarks and the precise ratio of the sub-atomic weight of hummingbirds.

—Nothing, says Yffat, is as it seems. Characters appear and vanish for no reason you can discern.

—You appear to be exactly as you seem.

—Your intelligence, she says, her hands in her hair, is faulty. Cherry-picking reality is fraught with complexities. A man passes gas in the Tokyo subway, and butterflies die by the thousands in New Mexico. When the butterflies are reborn someone will say, they can explain it. Why some people live backwards. Why there are signs on doors that say – caution doors alarmed; as if anyone would want to frighten a door.

I may love you both, you and Audrey, but you will end up being pitched off a roof or slitting your wrists. Or it will all be revealed, everything they have done and then there will be a revolution. But that is not like a movie. It is as if everyone has gone mad at the same time. And then you'll wish they had pitched you off a roof or you had slit your wrists when you had the chance.

—No one knows anything until it happens.

—It is the end of the world, she said, and no one is who they claim to be. You must understand time is unraveling. Time is always unraveling and reforming. It has seasons and flavors.

—I don't understand.

—You are living backwards just as much as forwards.

—I don't know.

—Many strange things occur that foolishly are dismissed as coincidences.

—Must we speak like this?

—We could, if you prefer, leave claw marks on the walls.

—What does it mean, if the system is consistent, it cannot be complete?

—It means, I would rather read Frank O'Hara with you, than do anything else. But it's too late.

—Why?

She stopped moving. She looked at me with her big brown eyes. Outside, the evening gathered in the corners of the city and gave marching orders to the day.

☙❧

Elements of the Narrative Appear at odd Angles like a Cubist Painting

Audrey with her hair up is a cameo and Reiko who will appear briefly without preliminaries and then vanish without explanation is standing naked before me, does not move as I focus and snap the shutter and capture some barely concealed place of her and her breasts stand like perfect tear drops and her smooth stomach curves down to the red-brown glory of her bush itself deeply scented curving around as a half-circle to the most delicate beauty of her exquisitely round ass rising majestically to the perfect arch of her back and not once did I touch her with my hands but ate her with my eyes and I enjoy her very much and sometimes ache at how this knowledge of her sex has placed me in the space that existed between her and her husband, Wayne, who has surrendered sadly to life and sells insurance and in the file I marked, Japan, that I keep in a drawer in my head, she is so obviously a type, a single, fragile, ancient, resilient sheet of paper upon which I drip cum and solution and enlarge until, in white and black she hangs upon my wall as a goddess, a totem, a dark skinned fetish for the dream of sex and this is what remains—a last piece of privacy leaking into a file in a warehouse with infinite shelves full of names.

ℰℛ

Dead or Alive

Everything begins to bleed. I am bleeding and the street and the sky and the cars the buildings and soon the color is drained from everything and no one speaks about it. We're walking down the street and a man says Jesus is coming brother and Audrey says everyone is so afraid.

✠✠

Necessary Tools

"From that point on, the extraordinary system of spies and informers which has played an important part in the political work of the French state into our own time took shape. (Sartine, who became lieutenant general de police in 1759, is supposed to have said to Louis XV, "Sire, when three people are chatting in the street one of them is surely my man.") Eighteenth-century police manuals like those of Colquhoun in England or Lemaire in France are no less than general treatises on the government's full repertoire of domestic regulation, coercion, and surveillance."

—Charles Tilly

✠✠

At the Augean Stables

I'm nearly broke and I'm standing in front of a beer-stenched bar on Geary Boulevard with all the professional drinkers. Patrick Toole is leaning over the split door entrance to the Horse's Hoof, his sweat-stained leather cowboy hat perched back a little and his face is all lines and furrows and deep chasms of time.

His small blue eyes are often cheerless even when he smiles and when he's been drinking they get empty except for violence that never comes but just goes down deeper with the booze and he lives in his van, is always kind to us, polite, and Audrey buys him an ice-cream cone from Jo's and we stand in front of the bar and eat ice-cream while the broken people come and go and in their faces every fear is branded, every piece of them leaks the fragile and drinking is all about being slow and the repetition of slowness and the same jokes and the same stories, the same gestures that are themselves epics of repetition and the sameness and the slowness are the attempt to arrest time and they stoke the engine of the bar and it chuffs the hours and the night is a *passionate nomad* full of passengers and many ripe oranges flutter in the dark and dead flowers roll up and down the sidewalk and the characters come and go regular as the tide and there's Mookie who sells weed for Mr. Jellybean and Mookie, he steers clear of Patrick because Patrick sees him clearly as a junkie punk always scamming, looking-stalking and Mookie's grandfather owns the camera store down the street but he's cut off from the family, grifts and has a friend called Lemon (because his skin has a yellow tint from a disease) but Lemon is big and menacing and Patrick is not big but is as menacing as a shark when he turns the small dead blue eyes in his knock-about skull at you and whirling in this infinity I feel lost and feel myself waiting only for the courage to walk to the bridge but I know Patrick Toole would never walk to any bridge but just might put his old marine .45 to his head if he ever found out he had cancer or some such thing and he wobbles on the edge of a razor between being and not but mostly he's just amber; frozen a broken watch, a true time machine because time is the crone in the corn stalks and she's just awful and Toole is an alcoholic and has a fine, fine box full of colored pencils and pastels, erasers and pencil sharpeners because he's an artist who never paints anything and his box of tools is always very neat, precise and orderly as soldiers on a parade ground, and he's often sitting in his van facing the bar staring over his troops, all clean and ready and he never summons them to battle because that war was fought and lost a long time ago and you can put a quarter in the Patrick Toole arcade and he springs to life and you can hear the stories about being in the Crotch, the Special Forces and drinking and whoring in Panama, but he's never told me a lie, and never been cruel and is always as generous as his wounds will allow and the other drunks are as frozen as he, all of them, beaten down into fractured submission and Toole's friend Paul is pious, goes to mass every Sunday, then to the bar and has a pace maker because he blew his heart out with speed and coke and now goes to the local pot club and buys and everyone smokes; the whole city is floating on a grayblue cloud and the scent is everywhere from the big bay windows to the fancy little disco cars where the good young Chinese boys light up before going into the video store to play electronic war and I'm a sponge unable anymore to unload or stop filling up and I want to rip my head off and drop kick it through the Gate or dribble it down the street screaming and I tell Audrey it feels as if I'm getting stiff, mummified-stiff and dead without the benefit of death only aware and stuck here with the *Ministry* at every turn, so that the only escape is to jump, or hang, or swallow and drown sleepy warm and float until everything goes away forever unless, as Jason the broken down actor (who hasn't acted professionally in thirty years) says: 'No, you'll just come back miles behind where you started this time and as horrible as it's been this go around it will be even worse next time', but he's a liar and a thief and his grandfather was a preacher and Jason says (repeating the epic story of his family) - the sunlight yellow (and again yellow-silver, tinted blue and fecund), stuttered through and reverberated off heavy Spanish Moss opening and closing cool shadows in the spring moist Georgia air and (whirlwind of movement) the long black car churned dust from the road under the trees till, stopping at a crossroads, Reverend O.W. Waters (or as the Congregationalists knew him Obadiah Waters 'Parting' Waters, so named for his Father Obadiah Ishmael Waters who married his cousin Mahalia Waters and who was himself born on February 19th and had a son who was himself born on February 19th and who himself had a son born on February19th) inhaled once and then set foot to gas then seeing the truck on his left stopped (again, exchanging brake for gas, apprehension for reality of blood and color) and the thinly veiled nervous twitch of eyes and tightening of face and fearful desires (thinking; long damp twine of moss living on but not parasitically from the trees) he placed one hand down on the knee of his grandson (Jason) and the other plainly on the top of the wheel and laid his gaze down at the nothing he conjured between the wheel and the dash and the quickly filling space of his chest (with beating heart and iron-taste of blood in his mouth) then heavy breathing dryness and tingling rushing adrenaline and in his ears the sound of the truck door opening and closing and the slow walk then seeing the big hands white on the black door of the car the narrow face (long, like the hardened rubber tip of a pencil bent just so slightly to the left as if while wet, a great and persistent force had leaned heavily on one side of the head, shifting nose and eyes and thin lips off center) and hearing the familiar voice and thick breath scented with gin and charcoal, that bespoke:

—*Boy,* (the voice, flinty, emerging from the dirt and endless time), did you not see me com'n down this road?

—Why yes sir, I did, said Parting Waters, I did see you.

—Then, *boy,* why did you co-*mence* to proceed?

—It is, sir, my right of way, and you are obliged by the law to yield.

—Obliged to yield, Precha? (asumption, yet correct for recognition of a type in a type of car and size and bearing and poise and knowledge and reading and writing and knowing what is revealed in a face and eyes...)

—Yes sir. And now I'm on my way to my congregation down the road.

— *Boy,* you go, if and when I say you can go.

—Well, now, said Parting Waters, a small pause

of enormous size dancing from his mouth, I don't exactly think that's the case, and his hand, as a sheet on a wire in a just heavy breeze rose from his grandson's knee and floated towards the glove-compartment, extended a long thick forefinger, tapped the button, once, (and the moist spring sweat of moss and trees, dirt and cars and breath, opened) and received softly with delicate menace, the metallic, click, of the springs on either side of the small platform and the hands of the bent-man now gripped tightly fear, the heat of the warm metal and rubber window frame and just crooked eyes blinked stinging small drops of sweat and saw the hand levitate again towards what darkness in the box and stop between being and not being and the thin tight mouth spoke slow words of departure and inside-out fear as bravado and the sudden ache of tightly constricted balls and sure knowledge of his wife needing to receive a lesson in care (and the beating when it came as it always came was sudden and desperate, hysterical (because she did not know that he had been humiliated) and hot like warm metal and cool after; dead without flow of blood like metal again and metal on the skin and the wife later with shaking hands twirled gently a strand of her long red hair around one forefinger and stared blankly, whispering desolate poems of fractured misery long long long hair is fine on a fine horse or (perhaps it was a dog), and she wondered after cause and effect thinking perhaps the cause for this beating was the piggy-faced man at the town market-store, whose ears enfolded in fat seemed unlike ears at all but were only pink labyrinths on the sides of his fat head and once throwing a knife on top of a nail barrel had insulted this rubber-headed man who as if directed by hands invisible went home and raped her, beat her and the rage of dust swirling in combat unknown and understood by neither the beaten or the one beating as a tide on any shore is only the tide endless and without self except as it is given by us to it and received in return as we abandon the self for unity with the all) and stepping back, walking-turning towards the truck said:

—You get on to that congregation if they wain'n on you, and watch where you go with a child in there and these few seconds stretched out and turned and became the days that became the years that were the blood in the deepest veins of the earth.

And then the door opening, closing, the motor starting the truck humping heavily on worn axles down the road went leaving behind a rising cloud of white exhaust splitting like a sheet on either side to leave the road clear while, with small brown-black eyes Parting Water's grandson watched the large soft hand retrieve from the glove-compartment a chrome-steel hammer held like a gun and turning looked up to see the Reverend laugh in nervous exaltation, an ocean of sweat pouring over his skin, and begin to drive down the road humming to himself and his vision of god.

ᢒᢒ

A Riff on the Nature of Time, Identity & Consciousness

"There is no such thing as the future and no such thing as the present; there is only the past happening over and over again right now."

— Eugene O'Neil

ᢒᢒ

Empire Snow

I remember Berlin, the empire snow heavy and the sky grey and the past which is present and the now which is forever and the monument to the wall buried under the snow so the long tail-fins of the cars shot out under the streetlights in shades of yellow-white and blue moist and dripping and I said this was the before, a life that was and remains, is, and the girl who asked about the past and the girl in what was then West Berlin became the before for the girl in the wine store who is un-named but asked about the past in the story about the girl asking about the girl and before Audrey asked about Berlin, Samantha asked about Audrey and someone (who remembers who because it really is all terribly confusing) asked about Samantha and the spies and the story unfolding tumbled out of darkness and the girl in Berlin came to Greece before we went to Berlin and thinking of her I wrote: *I could meet you on Naxos, sunset on Naxos, on jazzed water, and half empty streets... we sit quietly, with just empty glasses, the newspaper read twice...your name is unknown, as is mine. Not the given name, I mean the one that is taken, taken as a true name the title your lover gives you that is taken from you by your lover, the identity that is created...your face is hidden...your hands are small cats that rub against me, purr in mine, curl into my pockets and sleep there.*

☟☜

The accident begins in Athens. The taxi driver is a cheat... I know he is cheating me; this fat man who sweats in the ten-ton heat of the Greek fall. This fat man driving in a long lazy circle before heading out to Piraeus. He spins a rosary around one short fat finger... a thin stick figure hangs from the rear view mirror. The figure of a juggler set to juggle three balls held in place by thin wires attached to its wooden body... I look at the fat man. The sweat at the back of his neck rushing through the bright red creases of his skin.

He reminds me of the only important thing I ever learned in school. It goes like this: An ancient city has been unearthed. The ruins are six-thousand years old. Found are clay pots, silver coins, broken swords... and a pair of dice; six-sided dice made of ivory.

The dice are rolled and come up sixes. Both dice show six. The dice are rolled again. Again both show six. The dice are rolled one-hundred times. Each time, only sixes. These are cheater's dice. They are for deception, for victory in games of chance, where winning is an accident, losing a lack of experience. He is a cheater, this sweating fat man. I let him cheat. In six-thousand years, nothing has changed and the long lazy humid ride to Piraeus takes twice as long as it should or exactly as long as you would imagine.

The ferry for the island has just left. A mere, five minutes, says the fat man. He leans against the hood of his taxi, lights a cigarette, offers me one, shrugs his shoulders. A common gesture there. Everyone is always missing something, so a shrug of the shoulders to show a benign resignation, an acceptance of one's fate, one's accidents.

ॐॐ

I met her on Naxos. I was waiting for the bus, or rather, the driver who I had seen the day before, drunk, driving a tractor pulling a bed full of bales of hay. He drove wildly down the road and the hay fell onto the road and the next day waiting for him I thought, no, this is stupid, and I got off the bus and sat on a low brick wall looking over the harbor road.

It was early fall and the sea was a low, thrilling rush of electric blue being pulled like a sheet in the gathering warm wind. The Meltemi blew hard and then harder still and a white sandwich board fell down with a shot and I went to pick it up at the same time as a man in a white three-piece suit and dirty white shoes as if it were all an accident designed by fate.

His name he said was Nikos, and he handed me a card that said his name and the name of his club – Club Pegasus… Tonight, he said, you will come… it is the grand opening…

I was aware of and smiled at the wind as if it were a person and I was happy because I was a fool and didn't know any better and I saw he had dirty nails and his suit was a little dingy and I thanked him and we agreed to meet at a café on top of Saint Michael Square.

ᛰᛰ

Blue ink-spilled sky I waited at a table on the square drinking brandy and eating a plate of salted almonds, the square rolling along over the hill with chairs and tables all tilted one way or another a white washed chapel with a blue dome like a billboard for faith.

☞☜

The square was filling up with locals and tourists and Nikos came across the square in the same white suit and with him was a tan girl with long black hair.

Her name was Astrid and they lived together and we sat at the table and drank brandy and talked and Astrid was from Germany though she said her mother was from Brazil.

—Why are you come to Naxos? She said to me her leg pressed against mine under the table.

—I don't know, I said, feeling her leg warmly against mine. She smiled and ran one hand through her long black hair so that it was as if you were watching a wave rise and fall and her long neck was every shore facing the deepest sea.

☞☜

I is Another

Audrey naked on her stomach says call me by her name… tell me about her… tell me about her while they listen. Fuck me as if I am her while they listen… start at the beginning and concentrate. Who am I? Name me… the original of me… as if we had met in Greece…

☙ ❧

That is we

In the film I would get out of bed and light a cigarette, stand on the balcony looking pensive, wise, accidental, a world-weary young man of twenty-something in a dirty white shirt, a day's worth of stubble on my face.

But I do not smoke and the balcony looks unstable. I have a white shirt but it's clean. I am naked because of the heat. I do not need a shave.

The room I have rented for the night in Piraeus looks over an alley and the alley empties into a triangular lot. The side of the hotel faces two apartment buildings. There is a light on in one of the buildings. A single yellow square is formed by the light and behind it, a thin shadow moves back and forth. I close the shutters on the balcony, walk to the bathroom and turn on the light. The roaches that have come out to feed stop where the light has caught them. There are hundreds of them on the walls. For a moment they do not move and then as if they were a curtain they drop and forming a line, slip down the drain. I look at the faucet in the sink and a large brown and black roach drops shiny and wet from the tap and scurries across the basin to surf down the drain. It makes me smile.

☙

Later that morning I leave for the ferry. It is a short walk down to the docks. It is that part of the day when you can still pretend that time exists, retreat into the illusion that time is real. But time is not real. Along the docks, trucks are lumbering back and forth and scooters like loud roaches are racing down the crowded streets.

☙

You are on the beach looking up into a cloud that looks like a horse in a fresco on the wall of a church in Spain and in the film you are made to say: Isn't it funny that I'm never where I think I am? And turning to a man who is and is not me, who was and was not beside you on the shore below the low hill on which sat the small whitewashed church with the bright blue door: Hasn't anyone ever noticed that the wind only blows when the falling leaves are chasing each other?

☿☙

Pictures at an Exhibition

I am standing across the street from a movie theater. There is a fountain behind me and rising out of the fountain is an enormous sculpture with men in uniform hanging from a great flame and the plaque reads Katyan and across the street I watch the long line moving inside the theater to see the film about the lovers in Greece and when the wall came down and in the news there is the story about the man who wrote the film and he is not I and I is another and my words bleed inside his and the Ministry records and writes.

☿☙

The Rain

It was raining in the film made from the story made from the life that was the story being told and remembered. They stood in a half circle at one entrance to the Old Quarter of the town facing the back of a wooden cart. In the bed of the cart was a man sitting with ropes around him tied to the back slats of wood so that his torso was up and his legs were straight out, one normal-looking in dirty jeans and a work boot muddy and wet and the other broken with the thigh swollen so that his pants were stretched and his leg looked like the moist black body of a well-fed seal. His face was tight as if a clamp had been fixed to his skull. The lighting was sepia-toned and he was pale-looking, sweaty, heavy and jowl-thick with grey stubble and his eyes were small blue and fixed on some midpoint at the end of the bed while the rain fell on him and the people waiting with him standing there in the rain, none of them saying anything. An old man with a blue cap on his head and three women who turned red worry-beads in their thick hands waited before the film store where a man was using his developer to shoots x-rays while the light rain came down in thick silver strands that went surging down the narrow streets.

☙☙

It is a banal poignant brutality: The peasant farmer in the rain. He will walk for the rest of his life with a limp if he lives, and the elegant poetic terror of it leaves a scar on your memory.

☙☙

To Begin Again

Her name was Adiah, and angels and devils waged unending war in the curls of her long brown hair. I am speaking metaphorically. I am speaking metaphorically because she had sex with women. I am speaking metaphorically because she had sex with men. I mean everything and nothing, her long brown hair and her thighs, darkly curving below the thin fabric of her blue dress billowing in the late summer breeze.

☒☒

When I knew her in Jerusalem, before I was anyone, washed up on the shores of the city, impaled on the idea of the city with my identity broken, she was a thought, the lighthouse to which I should swim only to see her drift away again, and again.

Looking constantly for better light for her painting, for her anxiety, she moved every six months; a summer and fall in Talpiot, a winter and spring in Old Katamoun. She moved so often that soon she was able to begin a conversation in Rehavia, and end it in Bak'a.

☒☒

For me it was all always the same: The sight of her arriving, the idea of her leaving, the flower of her face, opening and closing.

❦

Once, she said to me defiantly, trying to shock me, trying to entice me, trying desperately to confuse me, she said to me, 'I made love to a Hasid once'.

Foolishly, crudely over the debris of lunch in the narrow alley near the bookstore where she worked within the liquid slowness of a summer afternoon, sitting outside at a small table in front of Ima's restaurant, I asked her how she had made love to him, and she said, in surprising modesty coming from somewhere that I did not know, hidden amid the white reeds and bulrush of her better self, softly, 'Don't ask me that', and it seemed to me then and has seemed to me ever since, that it was as if her whole being was suddenly visible there in her dark face, and it was as if her whole being was going to crack like a dry leaf and then it was gone, disappearing under the layers of bravado and coolly practiced cruelties that always entered sideways secretly, like a blind yellow-fish, and I was left to torture myself with the idea of him staining the dark map of her body.

❧ ☙

So, I imagined him. He was an overly serious, nervous man with chalk-white skin and delicate hands, who sweated too much in his rumpled black suit and black shoes, with squishy black socks, working himself like a piston in the engine-house of god, bouncing up and down in the ten-ton heat of a Jerusalem summer, small pieces of half-chewed prayers stuck to his greasy sweaty beard and pubic hair, a large Ethiopian family living in his hat.

But it was not as if I didn't know him. I did. I knew him by the hundreds, by the thousands.

I have seen him, at ten, or twelve, a pudgy child with a face set in the full bloom of arrogance and anger, fearful of being seen, desiring to be known. That face, unchanging, except for a beard, locked in place from birth, to death. Part of the vast army of black ants, he emerged every day from the nest, scurrying, able to lift ten times his own weight in prayers and the rules of the universe. I knew him.

Black ant of Me'a Sharim, sweaty hypocrisy and holy desire, tefillin of bondage, he comes coolly in his mind, god's gangster, enforcer for the messiah, but arrives instead, shaking, seeing her, overcome with want, eyes red-rimmed, he follows her, sees where she works, lives, waits until, like a dripping spoonful of blood and sperm, she sees him and invites him in to her, to her hands.

He comes to her. He shows her. He wants her to see him. She sits naked smoking, one leg crossed over the other, her foot, tapping the air then slowly, grinding the cigarette out into an ashtray on the low table in her apartment, she crosses her legs again and he sees her briefly, and she watches him and knowing her, I see her imagine being watched; strangers, listening to them.

He comes to her once, twice, three times, like a clock running backwards, running down, then he races, goes as fast as he can to Tel Aviv, to the whores there rather than in Jerusalem to make his shame as he calls it, correct. He never sees her again. She's not ever sure of his name. He could have told her anything, and what difference would it have made to her; to either of them?

So it goes. He disappears. It's as if he had never been. People forget if his beard was black or red, if he was tall or short. They forget about his delicate white hands, his thin fingers like pieces of chalk. When he dies, all the paintings, the photographs, are turned towards the walls. Clothes are torn. For seven days everyone weeps, stares blankly.

Later the paintings, the photographs are turned back, dusted, and when no one is looking, the clothes are sewn like small wounds being healed. It's as if he never existed.

Later still further along within the story, leaving her garden apartment with its mint plants, leaving her hash pipe and her constellation of cats, smelling her on my fingers not wanting to wash, I walked home alone in the late blue of the day, the trees clicking their dry summer bones, and in the stillness of my room limp and erect in my mind at the thought of her, I watched the curtains in front of the small balcony glide back and forth. The day breathed in quietly exhaled, and was done.

The Transparency

This is how the film begins; with the dark room. This is how everything begins. Time stops, becomes memory. Memory stops, becomes Adiah, becomes history. I hear the nameless narrator, who is Joshua, who is supposed to be me, speaking over the camera as it races over the electric blue of the sea around the island, say: I could meet you on Naxos, sunset on Naxos, on jazzed water, and half empty streets... we sit quietly, with just empty glasses, the newspaper read twice...your name is unknown, as is mine. Not the given name, I mean the one that is taken, taken as a true name, the title your lover gives you, that is taken from you by your lover, the identity that is created...your face is hidden. Your hands are small cats that rub against me, purr in mine, curl into my pockets and sleep there...

☞☜

So, in the film, Adiah, who is Yffat, imagined, portrayed by someone else, rises from the bed, naked, lights a cigarette. It is a warm evening in the perpetuity of video and the windows are open against the heat. A radio is on, playing a piano concerto, but it's never completely clear. I mean the music is never completely clear, interrupted by static drifting in and out it is, as if someone else was always trying to be present, trying to be heard or recognized and the music and the static form a variation that repeats.

There is someone else in the room but we can't see them. There is only a dim outline, a shadow; and smoking, she speaks softly and all of the images, one after another spill out, blur, the illusion of time, the line between past and present.

A television is on but without the sound. The image of the screen repeats throughout the film, over and over again pretentiously, the television is shown, and on the screen of the television, we see the same scene repeated again and again.

The television is showing an old film being run by a station in Cairo. It is grainy black and white, and the images jump, jiggle. Scratches race by like great hairy bugs and the images keep repeating. Prelude to the revolution that must fail.

A boy looks up. The film cuts suddenly to a group of men in a large well-furnished colonial-style house with tall white columns. The house is filled with antiques. The men are standing in a large library. A short fat man in a wrinkled white suit has his hands on a large globe set in an ornate wooden brace. The men run from the house. They run outside to a dusty, circular driveway. They run for two impossibly large American sedans from the nineteen-forties.

The cars are immense, jet black with running boards and great bulbous headlights. They look, ominously, like obese wasps.

The men pile into the cars. One of them jumps on the running board of one of the cars, and the cars speed away, sending a great cloud of dust into the air.

The man on the running board is trying to hold on but he can't. He rises, lifts off from the side of the car, falls to the ground rolls, comes to a stop, flat on his back stunned.

He lifts himself from the ground, turns towards the camera, and waves his hands frantically in the air; seems to scream, even as the cars race off down a long dirt road, lined with tall palm trees.

Then, as the man stands, pointing and screaming

at the camera, the film spools back again. The boy looks up, the men race from the house, run to the cars with the great protruding headlights, and speed away.

The man on the running board lifts off again, is hoisted up and away by gravity, is thrown to the ground rolls, comes to a stop, lifts himself up, waves his hands in the air, and screams, frantically, into the camera. He screams because, it's all a terrible accident. I mean, he has become a terrible accident. His identity has been reduced, transformed, into an accident. The accident begins, the accident ends, and he simply continues.

And in the dark room, where the television is on, without the sound, I see Yffat, who is Adiah sitting up in bed, then standing, lighting a cigarette, the windows open, the curtains drifting back and forth, on the leaden evening heat.

There is a lot of smoking. Everyone's always reaching for a cigarette, lighting a cigarette, blowing smoke from a cigarette, grinding out a cigarette. Everyone's bored, nervous, languid, depressed, and it's true.

I watched the film. I watch it again. I see her, Yffat, see her run her hand down the middle of a woman's back, slowly, with great and deliberate care, her fingers unfurl, like small flags, or ideas, until she is running them all along the woman's back, then curling, retreating, she begins to write with her forefinger only, letters, on the skin of the woman beside her.

The film breaks, all of a sudden; cuts to a black screen and the first of a series of quotes appears:

"To remember the dead is to betray them."

The film returns and the woman, whose face we cannot see: we hear her. We hear her as she guesses what is being written on her, each letter, each word, one by one, the letters repeated, until she laughs, then, understanding the message, she says a name suddenly, as if she were surprised, hurt, happy to have discovered the truth.

And in the end, the woman, who is Adiah and Yffat leaves, disappears. Almost as if she were dead or almost dead, she turns, walks away, up into a tower on a Greek island, like some kind of later-day celluloid-Circe, the camera turning around and around, then the tracking shot of the sea, birds wheeling overhead...

ᔕᘻ

I sit for hours by the fountain. The night walks by in many forms. After the movie a couple comes out of the theater. They stand under the marquee. They talk and then the woman answers her phone. She looks at me. They walk towards the fountain and they stare at me and then they come and sit across from me.

They are silent and there is the sound of the cars and the water and fragments of conversation and then the man says to the woman, 'I like the girl in the film and how the man says angels and devils waged unending war in the curls of her long brown hair' and the woman stares at me and she says 'and the scene with the crazy drunk painter Jorge and the beautiful Japanese girl having her portrait done'.

They stare at me. I stare at them. The statue in the fountain is painted in shades of faded gold and the patina is blue-gray and the water in the depth of the lights that ring the fountain is brightly white and streaked with silver.

I stand and walk across the street and I look back and the woman is speaking on her phone and they are staring at me.

∽∾

Complexity and Complexity

Samantha demands that I admit that life is not complicated; that it is, as she says, 'what we make of it'. I smile at her. I want to explain. I can't. Or rather I can only shrug my shoulder and say once I knew a girl in Jerusalem and there were spies and the *Ministry of Ambiance* has many deep tunnels but she does not want to hear and she says the plums will never kill themselves but I know better and watch the birds drifting back and forth in orderly gusts of feathers fanning in the twilight tremble.

ஜஜ

Ideas of Order

Samantha sits behind the wheel of her car looking out the window. A possum waddles out of the small copse of trees. We watch it and wonder together what it means. It is late and we are sitting in the parking lot of the dreary old Braddock building and she has been asking me to tell her about Audrey.

ஜஜ

Audrey emerges from the sea dripping and tan, her blonde hair slick down her back; and down the curving beach slick on the low cliff, the waves splash against the stone stairs leading up and down from a small white washed chapel.

ஜஜ

Maryanne emerges from the sea dripping and tan, her short blonde hair slicked back on her head and her brown eyes fiercely full of joy and love; and down the curving beach, slicked on the low cliff, waves splash and together on the beach, close to each other, she whispers to me, hasn't anyone ever noticed the leaves…?

✄ ✄

Club Pegasus opened to a few wastrel tourists and a howling wind that leaves the patio with its bright opening night banners in a jumble of tilted plastic chairs and wires twisted around each other and Astrid bitterly resigned, confides her disappointment saying who opens a club in the fall…?

✄ ✄

She enters in a pair of ballet flats, a tight black dress and a black scarf around her neck. Her blonde hair is short and slicked back and she walks to me at the bar. She leans close and whispers,

—This man is following me; he won't leave me alone. Will you pretend you know me?

I agree to pretend and that is real and false as one exchanges places with the other and she says her name is Maryanne.

I bought her a drink and we stepped outside and from within the surging wind on the patio, the sound of the waves bruising the shore, I looked past her and saw a local looking forlornly after her. He was a Niko, a fisherman with a dirty cap in his hands and dirty boots and a thick twice-broken drinker's nose.

She smiled half-heartedly at me.

—Do you always whisper?

—Yes, she said, leaning close and whispering.

I didn't ask her why. We talked, casually about this and that. She was from Berlin. She was on vacation. She was forty. I was twenty-four. Things came and then they went and I did not know that sometimes the truth may only come once.

☙☙

Three Days

1.

A mattress on the floor of a rented room in a new whitewashed building near the beach. Books in a small alcove. Her bag. A pair of sandals like the skeleton of a shoe, or a poem by Amicahi. A bathing suit hanging in the small shower. She is tan and tall, has small breasts and strong thighs. That night she wears nothing, except the black scarf. She whispers.

℘℘

2.

Breakfast outside on the patio of a *taverna* at the end of a narrow road that runs between a grove of lemon trees. A starkly blue sky without clouds above whitewashed buildings and the electric blue of the sea. The buildings all have one floor jutting out unfinished; iron rods protrude like broken bones.

—To avoid the tax, she says, laughing softly. If a house is finished there is a crippling tax so, they leave them like this. I like them like this: ugly, broken and interesting. Do you know Durras; The Lover is a great book you must be reading it now. Everything is always *memento mori*.

An old woman who looks as if she fell off a charm bracelet stands in the doorway to the kitchen, cleaning her teeth with a steak knife showing us a face mashed by time. She looks at us. Her eyes are without warmth. In the distance, the sea waves in and out as a clock and the heat drifts lazily in the air thick with the scent of the ocean and lemons.

I ask about the scarf. She stares at me directly, her eyes large and brown and soft. Cancer, she says; it never metastasizes, but returns again and again. Once a year she goes to her doctor and they find a new growth and they remove it and every time they do they take a little more of her voice.

Welcome, she says, to the cliché of your very own Euro-Indie-film.

☙❧

Her friends, a knot of wealthy Germans, are hosting a party in the old castle above the town. They have a villa at the top of the hill facing a courtyard with a broken fountain and an olive tree.

It is a warm evening at the end of fall and the square is full of people and tables piled with food and wash basins full of ice and beer and bottles of wine. Someone is strumming a guitar. Laughter opening and closing as fireflies turning on and off in the dark, lights strung from the building casting shadows in blue and green and she is wearing the tight short black dress. Her smooth skin is brown and electric, thrilling to the touch. Watching her from across the square, we share an open secret.

A man sits down next to me. He hands me a glass of wine. She turns and I watch her speaking with a woman who is looking at me over Maryanne's shoulder.

—I am Vladimir, says the man.

He sips his wine and looks at the women. Before us on the table, the food is shattered, scattered on plates, the plates scattered on the tables and there are bottles and a wedge of cheese with a long knife next to it and the blade is streaked with oily white smears.

—You've got a live one, he says and drinks.

I drink and watch his hands.

—A young man and an older woman is one of the better stories; so full of riotous luscious predictability. It is a kind of precise formula.

He put his glass on the table and reached for a bottle. He poured wine and drank it and he wagged the bottle at me and then without my answering, he tipped the bottle and poured more wine into my glass.

—Once when I was younger and a student in Madrid I met a woman; older, divorced. She was my friend's mother's friend. All the clichés; a house for the summer and so on. She was just what you would expect. And then after everything was good and I was getting my appetite for everything, her ex-husband's friends came. They spoke to her. I listened through a heating vent between rooms. Money owed and something about a boat and bank accounts and doing a favor and later, her crying on my shoulder and the most fevered sex and so on and I wrote a book about it, a memoir they'd call it now, but then we just called it a story.

I stared at him. He had vast spatulate fingertips and they gripped the glass tightly and spread out like the digits of some impossible amphibian with a taste for cheap table wines and drunken confessions.

He leaned in and his wine-breath, sour acid grape decayed, washed over me.

—There's a scene; very dramatic. The hero has just fucked the beautiful woman. Made ridiculous promises. He is standing on a balcony smoking. It is that insanely warm sensuous fabric we have here in the summer draping itself over you with the slow heat and all at once out of what seems nowhere the ex-husband's friends are on the balcony and in the film you see the cigarette fly into the air and tumble down to the ground and you are brought around to look up and there is our hero being held right over the railing.

He stopped and looked at me. He paused and someone came and took a bottle from the table. Maryanne was still with the woman who was looking from her glass to me and back again.

—Well, said Vladimir, I have talked too much or not enough.

He drained his glass and stood. He leered at me and his eyes were red and tired. He fished a cigarette from his shirt pocket and lit it with a lighter he took from his pants and then he blew an extravagant cloud over my head. He looked at me and he moved his free hand through the smoke.

—Like ending a service, he said, Go with god, yes.

He laughed and walked away and I watched him walk down the alley away from the square and I sank down into myself and watched a fat blue-streaked fly barrel-roll over the table and land on the knife blade.

☒☒

Leaving, we walk through dark alleys and stop and pressing her against the wall, I kiss her because I am desperate and want to believe nothing is true and her breath comes twice; once from her mouth and again from beneath her scarf. She pulls away but takes my hands in hers and we walk through a tunnel beneath the castle and emerge on a thin flight of stone stairs leading down towards the harbor and behind us up into the alleys of the old fortress. We push and pull and stop and kiss, her tongue wrapped around mine in deep scents of sharp crisp white wine full of citrus and apples and cigarette smoke her breath heavy with mine heavy and fast and pressing against her she says, here, now.

Then she pulls away and I follow her around a bend in the alley and she stops in front of an iron gate. Above and beyond it, is the last tower of the castle. She steps forward and climbs over the gate and I follow her to a round platform beneath the wall of the tower.

She leans against the wall and pulls me to her

and I press against her and against the tower wall and we turn and turn again and behind us the town tumbles down the hillside down and down towards the harbor lit and glowing yellow-white and the sea shadow-thick and turning, I have her against the tower and the thousand year old stones lifting her dress and she pulls at my belt, her voice whispering and I am inside her thrusting in against her and the wall and she stops moving and leans impassively there and I hold her tightly, our breath heavy-thick and fast, faster still until I empty myself in her and shaking leaning against her unmoving, her face blank and she is staring out past me down to the sea.

ᛞᛞ

A Kind of Invention

I am, said the voice in the film, always remembering you. A kind of invention. Half empty streets, remembered, invented, as being half full... I am always inventing you. I met you on Naxos. A black scarf, a party in the old, ruined fortress above the town... the curve of your back. The deep line...

I go high up into the hills above the town. I follow the trails through the dull gray rocks, running past yellow weeds to a plateau. An old man and woman are there working the vines. Thinking me Italian, he questions me, but I do not understand him... his face sags, he smiles, toothlessly, and gives me a handful of fresh grapes, black with dirt, a small plastic bottle of water.

—Always best, he says, slipping into broken English, to wash before you put it inside.

Further on, I begin to come down, down into the fields cut like steps into the mountain side. The ground is soft, warm, red. The sky immense, sharply vague, I lay down inside a ruined farm house, feel myself sink into the soft carpet of sheep shit and wash the grapes.

I eat them, feel their seeds, their juice on my lips. I think of her. My hands are sticky in the heat, and between the brown of the floor and the blue expanse of the sky, I release myself quietly, pouring out, thinking of her and the unmatched beauty of a moment alone without anyone listening.

☙❧

That famous European film

—What, she says, will you do?

We are sitting at a table in front of a *taverna* waiting for the ferry. It is late and the promenade is quiet. Fishing boats rise and drop on the late evening tide.

—I'm supposed to be writing a novel.

—Oh, she says pretending to be full of ennui, not another novel about someone trying to write a novel.

—I'm being watched.

—Of course you are, she says, everyone is being watched. It's what they do.

—They say you should write what you know.

—What the hell, she said, do *they* know?

ℬℜ

Indulge in a fine mint

"Each idea is already a memory and every memory leads inevitably to the next idea. Thus we are in two places at once and each identity is an ocean upon which we are lost always. But at least there is the scent of the lemon trees, exactly as you describe them; and still the weather here is luxurious and I find myself enjoying to indulge in a fine mint while all around me spies and their informants ask the most obvious questions."

— Lesharc A. Koffkalt
— Letters to Cavafy

ℬℜ

Only the Past

She stopped in the middle of the room, turned and I stood there looking at her. She walked to me and I put my arms around her and we kissed. I kissed her, and everything began again.

✍ ☙

A flock of small birds, gray crosses, rise turn descend. The night is a blue guitar. She is and is not opening and closing her face the flower of what what not hard soft oh and oh her brown belly then white but before my face to her thighs sweat spoons shoes cigarettes cars rain streets crowded and alone, commas, the solitary drops of rain books opening and closing time death a certain perfection saxophones cellos in blue a woman pregnant statues the day in the closed rain she tastes sharply of prayers chewed slowly but salt and sharp she writhes says oh oh make me sharply curling black tangle of sharply curling whisker-like hair the small nub stiffly rising emerging peeled open revealed I suck kiss tap with my tongue the code of desire listen please make me her hand in my hair I eat her naked bird-face she rises and falls I worship her spill myself on her and live briefly in the deep black surging moss of her dazzling electric fur and fog and drift and drift away a reluctant cloud.

ꙮ ꙮ

In the dark, where the light from the street stopped, she said, I thought, I mean, I imagined, I dreamed, I made you pregnant.

—With?

—Me.

ꙮ ꙮ

In the morning, she was gone and I sat alone, on the balcony, drinking a cup of instant coffee. She had forgotten her lighter. I sat there, the coffee in one hand, the lighter in the other. I ran the flame up, and down, and watched the morning traffic going back and forth. I thought about Adiah. I thought about Maryanne. I reread a letter from Audrey.

I looked down the street to where it curved and below the street, the small valley opened and startled by something I could not see, a crow shot upwards and turned once, twice, three times and came down without flapping its wings and settled silently back among the trees.

ꙮ ꙮ

3.

The ferry pulls away from the harbor in a surging rush of jittery surging blue and white tumbling water. I stand and watch and wait and she is going and I am staying and this was only three days and somewhere between crone and lover and both at once she is one and the same and I loved her and did not love her and the ferry, in deepening dark, slips further away and all at once, the lights snap on and the ferry is become a long line of blue and green and flashing yellow so much, so so very very much so love going and not yet done and you could never tell the story in one line that went from beginning to end and instead you walked in a circle and one moment became the next like the ocean, formed but shapeless.

☙❧

An Ornament of God

In Jerusalem I knew Adiah. She sits cross-legged on the brick wall of the balcony. She is smoking. Her wild hair flares out like an ocean or three ideas.

—Tell me, she says, sending a stream of blue-grey smoke into the bright blue air, about Greece and your German girl.

I laugh and lean over the wall and looking down at the street, I watch three religious girls in head scarves and sensible shoes walk silently in a row past the house.

∅ ℞

My Barbaric Yawp

"...why should god not appear to a starving man, as a loaf of bread..."

— Mahatma Gandhi

Why is this not a good argument for intelligent design? How is this not Indian mystic jazz riffing on the Eucharist?

∅ ℞

One day, in the mail, I receive a stack of postcards from Ariel. The first one is from Paris. He says he is giving a lecture. The card shows the Pont Des Artiste. His lecture is a big success. He says he had spoken in detail about how all works of literature are essentially forgeries.

In the second card, he is writing from Athens. He says with exuberance he has had dinner with his Russian-Greek translator; he's written a book made into a film – about a young man on a Greek island who has a torrid affair with an older woman who is blind. Homer! He writes in our time a modern Circe-Tiresias!

In the third one, he is in North Africa and he says he is chasing a woman; a writer he says; a hot fusion he calls her; twins he says, she's a twin!

He ends by saying, he hopes I will consider his offer of a job.

I sit on the floor and put the cards down in front of me and stare at them and the room grows dark and the minutes slip by and then the hours, and then the phone rings. I stare at it. It rings seven times and I wait and it stops. Then it rings again. I get up and answer it and there is dead air. I listen and then the line cuts off and eventually there is the recording of a voice saying – if you wish to make a call…

☏☏

The Chain

Audrey betrays everything. We are sitting in a café at the bottom of Thomas Street. The café is decorated with old toys and new toys are for sale and there is an ice cream counter and people sitting on the bench outside drinking coffee, and it is a pleasant evening at the end of Indian summer.

Two agents from the *Ministry* walk into the café. The man is young and fit; lithe and dark. The girl is fat and ugly with a face like the bottom of a well-worn shoe. The man walks to the counter and examines his cell phone and the sow drops her vast ass onto the bench close to Audrey and falling down on it she makes Audrey bounce and we look at each other and listen to these two whores from the Jerusalem branch of the *Ministry* repeat and echo the conversations Audrey and I have had in what is supposed to be the privacy of our home.

We sit for a moment and the stupidity of it, the embarrassing mongoloid performance art of it leaves us cold and depressed and frustrated and leaving, we walk up Thomas street without speaking until Audrey says they came out of the dance studio across from the café.

I ask her if she's sure and she's insistent and I begin to ask what she saw and when and what else she saw and the story begins to unravel and it is as if she were suddenly a spy spying on herself and caught behind a wall she had built and I cannot understand and we stand in the foyer of our apartment and she becomes adamant and remote and I am begging her to just tell the truth and the truth is that she has lied – she saw nothing, but lied and she lied about the lie and I beg her to understand that it might very well get one or both of us killed or worse and she

91

laughs defensively, saying, what could be worse than that.

—Do you not understand what is happening? Time is unraveling.

She stares at me, her face completely, impassively blank.

—They are spying on us; on everyone. It is not a joke; it is not make-believe. It is a narrative that is eating itself. It is a virus.

She stares and the dim recessed yellow light of the foyer casts her white skin in ivory with a blue tint. Her eyes are grey, her lips tightly pressed together. The lights make a persistent low hum.

—If you say the wrong thing, if you give me a lie and it leads to the wrong place, we could end up being trapped; arrested. It would be worse than being dead. If you're dead they can't hurt you anymore. We have to get out.

She continues to stare. She says nothing and stares blankly. I have the nearly uncontrollable urge to grab her and slam her head into the wall.

—Do you believe it's not true?

—No.

—Do you believe it is true?

—Yes.

—Then why would you lie?

She falls back into silence. We stare at each other. The light hums. Cars go by slowly on the street.

Somewhere in the apartment building water rushes through a pipe.

☞☜

Scalia, a King of Infinite Space

"Many think it not only inevitable but entirely proper that liberty give way to security in times of national crisis that, at the extremes of military exigency, inter arma silent leges. Whatever the general merits of the view that war silences law or modulates its voice, that view has no place in the interpretation and application of a Constitution designed precisely to confront war and, in a manner that accords with democratic principles, to accommodate it."

— Antonin Scalia

☞☜

At the Movies Everything is Bigger

Yffat works for a film company that is a front for the Ministry. She is making a documentary on the career of Mahmoud Mahaliwag, so, of course, *The Ministry of Ambiance* concludes that the documentary is a front for smuggling the secret of Katzenberg's Super Atomic Piston Ring and so they infiltrate their infiltration squad neither knowing the other exists and so: Fade in: A long distance view of a fog heavy city, faintly yet recognizably imperial though somehow rundown in a charming 19th century sort of manner; Durrell's Alexandria, Cairo, Istanbul, Amsterdam, Prague and Saint Petersburg all come to mind; a slow moving tram, shooting off sparks in the mist, corpulent even porcine and menacing leather-coated cops and paramilitary types with machine guns slung low and low slung eyes... a vast city, a megalopolis humming with action and ennui, vitality and ossification, a clogging of the arteries even as it spreads itself to the uttermost edges of... Labyrinthine city, cobblestone alleys, a wide cornice and whole streets made from pressed garbage that smolder perpetually as gasses are leaked and eventually, the streets suffer collapse only to be rebuilt, and packs of dogs small with thin tails, and in the rain, the sidewalks run black with soot and building-sized electronic billboards quiver and hum vibrating with orgasmic vitality and masturbatory indulgence, towering over the ancient river upon which the city, being wholly real, was built and the river is recognizable as a recognizable symbol of our self-conscious self–reflection and the camera work, steady and sure is exquisite and dead and in the editing room, inhaling at every turn Yffat's scent and (Audrey's perfume on her skin and in her hair),

I listen to her sigh, smoke a cigarette half-full with pot, and laugh at the director's view: God and pickles, as she often said for no reason that was ever explained to me, can you believe the people they give grants to? And then she turns dials and switches, and the images of the city move forward and backward, come into focus and disappear in a pixilated smudge... and reappear and on the screen, brown-red and seeming to move, the river lay curving between its banks like an exposed vein where boats and small tourist ferries moved and the city went on in cumbersome monotony from century to century and advanced in cumbersome monotonous distilled geometric and anti-geometric angles of gray and red and sometimes yellow and even there, on the 18th floor of the Shepherd's Hotel, it went on in noise, such noise—car horns, car alarms, sirens, explosions, jackhammers, gunfire, electric saws, fucking, screaming, barfing, farting, chewing, collapsing, hammering, whispering, torturing, filming, recording—to film the last interviews with Mahaliwag to sew up the documentary for the film festival— oh, Mahmoud Mahaliwag the *Sheik of SinEma*, the legendary godfather of film: 300 movies, 33 records, a book of poems, appearances, advertisements for coffee, tea, cigarettes, cigars and cigar-bars, wine and wine-clubs, nightclubs, banks, scotch, lottos, deodorants, toothpastes, breath-mints, colognes, racing teams of cars and horses, football clubs, department stores, car companies, orthopedic beds, hair transplants, nips, tucks, lipo-suctions, calling plans, health insurance, mineral waters and sodas, health clubs, computers, cell phones and airlines, cameras, film labs, digital cameras, camera-phones, smart-phones, dumb-phones, The Ministry of Tourism, beers, pens, cruise ships, hotel chains, video games, schools for the blind, the lame, leper colonies, haberdasheries, humus... etc, etc, etc....

Mahmoud on the set of Omdurman—The Greatest Epic ever produced. A cast of millions. A story of Empire, intrigue, romance... with Dean Hawk as young Lt. Churchill, Claire West as, Jenny, Gamal Sadat as the Mad Mhadi and Mahmoud Mahaliwag as... as...

Here comes everyone, he says to Yffat, waving one pudgy hand in the air as the entourage, replete with agents, reporters, handlers, spies, snitches, gangsters, an actress of indeterminate chemical origin, rolls into the grandly ornately dilapidated lobby of the hotel while boys in faded livery stand and watch, and the man from The Ministry watches everything and in his glasses are a small camera... and everyday Mahaliwag appears in the lobby of the hotel ready to tape the interviews that never occur because there's always something—a crowd arriving, departing, a wedding, a funeral, a woman, (perhaps two) and Yffat sits politely day after day withering away her grant money feeling the heat of dark eyes rolling over her delicious body and the air is a net of stagnated desire while every day Mahaliwag arrives charming and absent in costumes recounting each film, or commercial or his start in radio broadcasting singing ditties from English to Arabic back and forth, forth and back until, *How do I like My Hobart's tea—Hoot-Hoot-Ahhhhh,* becomes, *Ah, Mrs. Hobart, She has great bags,* and, *Wiggle-Wiggle Cigarettes from Ceylon* become, *Long Stick for your Pleasure Mouth* and Mahaliwag says—there, right there, says, in the costume of a 19th century Hussar—I met him there and he said I could make much better money working for him as, as... he waves a hand in the stale air and Yffat says: We're you an... operative? And Mahaliwag laughs while she sees the cavalry through the window ride by in great pomp and circumstance of blood and Yffat is suddenly wearing a long white dress that is uncomfortably tight and makes her look uncomfortably like an anorexic wasp, her parasol stinger at the ready but then, Mahaliwag is back and the drunken boat of time crests a wave and descends into the trough of the next moment and they continue...

—My dear it was all so long ago. But yes, I was recruited at Cambridge. I worked first as a translator and then I was transferred to the Queen's Art History

Department. Beautiful pieces came by me every day.

—Did you ever question your choice?

—At first certainly, but you know how it is; we have gulags, they have gulags. Theirs are internal while we, what's the phrase—we out-source them. We support dictators, they support dictators. The things we own are made by slaves. They spy on everyone. They infiltrate everything. So we spy on everyone and we infiltrate everything and together they have a vast library where they have a window that looks upon another room where there is a window that looks upon another room and they go on forever and in each room there is a list of everyone on the planet and every conversation is recorded and they take certain words and they put them in another room and they write a story and if at the end of the story your name is found, then they come to take you away and it is as if you were never alive. No one remembers your name; if you were tall or short.

—Your name was never on the list.

He laughed and smiled and looked her up and down.

—Oh no, my dear. My name has appeared on the list so many times I've lost count.

—Then they arrested you?

—I've been arrested a thousand times and tortured for an eternity and they keep coming to the end of the story and just as they are about to pronounce judgment someone always enters the room and they whisper and they confer and then they add a new name to the list and they add another chapter to the story and everything repeats.

—Everything repeats, then what's the point?

—Oh my dear that's just it. Knowing that the story keeps repeating does not give you an exit ramp, no it does exactly the opposite. It traps you. Knowing you are a character in a story only makes it worse because then you know you are trapped. And then you see that the threads intersect and reform and cross each other endlessly.

—This story is a jumbled, convoluted mess. How can you expect anyone to follow it?

—Always my dear, always.

—How do things work?

—Many strange things occur that foolishly are dismissed as coincidences and those looking for narrative cohesion instead of a representation of ideas linked thematically—as if fragments of consciousness did not move by leap-frogging over sequences in space-time, sometimes appearing as *before* and other times appearing as *after*—should look elsewhere along the narrative line. But of course even that is already in the script and I am just reading my lines.

—Isn't that fate?

—Who remembers my dear, who remembers? If the system is consistent, it cannot be complete. If it is complete, it will be inconsistent.

—Is that *our* fate?

—Who knows my dear, who knows...

He smiled and asked the waiter to bring them tea.

ඥ ඥ

But this position, this arch self-consciousness is just another moment... you see, there, it fades, goes out... in the film, about us... we watch ourselves played by people like ourselves... Yffat laughs, she says, because she knows with certainty that the funniest place you can go is a cemetery.

—If it doesn't make you laugh, she says, you have no sense of things.

—Do you believe in fate?

—Wars come and go. War is apparently forever.

—Does everything repeat?

—Another date with that cliché history.

—I don't understand it.

—How many times must we have this conversation.

She smiled and ran her hands through her hair.

ඥ ඥ

To Berlin

I am in Jerusalem talking to Michael about Adiah and Maryanne and about going to meet her in Berlin and in my pocket, I have a letter from her scented with her perfume and Michael and I are sitting on the patio at the front of his apartment drinking tea.

This is a chapter in the story that is about the story and Michael is a character in the story and he will appear and vanish without explanation as in life, as if you could read a stage direction that said: Enter, stage left, Michael, to the narrator.

—Berlin, he says and laughs. That's fantastic.

—Seems fantastic. Seems unreal.

—A beautiful girl in Berlin, in winter. What's not fantastic about that?

—I don't know. I think there's a tap on the phone.

He sips his tea. In front of us is a mint plant and beyond the plant, there is a small knot of tall pine trees and across from the patio to his left, a flight of stone stairs leads up to the street. It is October and warm during the day and cold and getting colder at night and the sky is precise and clear and full of many stars brightly bright and gleaming like impossible ideas.

—Of course, he said, the *Ministry* thinks you're a punk. The kind they want to hire.

I looked at him. He was thin then, deeply down

in the grips of his austere vegetarian phase and his eyes were sunk in and his cheeks were steeply drawn and his thick black hair was long and he wore it in a long tail that trailed down to the middle of his back.

I sipped my tea. We were sitting on rattan chairs with a wicker table between us. The light above the front door was on and I watched a moth flit back and forth between the growing dark and the light cape that fell from the bulb.

—You go to see her, they'll think you're doing something; that you're chasing something other than pussy. Everyone invents the truth.

—They suffer from an excess of too much imagination. Eventually they will go away; no?

—They suffer in a wilderness of shadows. But they remember forever. Institutional memory is eternal. They'll remember you, me, Adiah. It's forever. There is a library somewhere and in it everything is recorded. It is the infinite library of everything.

—It's all so pointless.

—Everything repeats. That's why it is not pointless.

I stared at him. He stared at his cup of tea.

—You could always not go, he said, but then you'd be a double dumbass. Besides, you have to go. Even though it will change things.

—How's that?

—A dumbass screws up but doesn't know. He's perhaps the fool, well-intentioned but unformed. A double dumbass knows better but screws up all the same. You don't want to be him.

—No.

—Of course you don't want to be that man. Who does? I've known both. When I was in the army there was this kid, I mean we were all young and stupid but he was happy, he had bought the package and we were up in the mountains and it was beautiful. Snow was on the highest peaks and below, all the way down the hills, you could see the ocean.

He leaned back and cracked his back. He turned his neck from side to side. It sounded as if someone was stepping on peanut shells.

—We parked our tanks near a monastery. That was in the winter. In the morning, the monks came out in a procession. I used to think if I were a writer I would write it. In the morning sometimes, when it was still dark, it was very cold and they looked like moths in their brown robes waiting for the sun to warm them so they could fly away.

He sipped his tea and curled his legs in under himself. A car drove by slowly and birds moved in the dark upper branches of the tallest trees.

I turned and watched the moth. It landed on the light and flew away and circled jaggedly back into the dark and then came back again and I saw it move to the light and go away again.

He looked at the moth and smiled. He shrugged

his shoulders.

—It's nice when that happens, he said, like god is listening and adding a footnote note to what you're saying. As if we needed stage directions.

I nodded and looked back at the moth. Michael began talking again.

—There was the cold rain after the winter. There was mud everywhere. That's when the rats came. They were big and there were so many of them. We started shooting them and that went on for a while until they said it was a waste of bullets so we stopped and there were just rats everywhere. The noble kid, the one who was a true believer, he had this thing about the rats. He got white and got the shakes when he heard them squealing. It was the strangest thing to see and we were all together in this tent. The other guys—they were scared all the time. So they took it out on the guy with the rat problem. They spoke with their voices high like rats. They made squealing sounds and you could see it was making him crazy. But he was always the first one up and out and not because of what they were doing but because he believed. Then when they didn't get a response, they killed a rat, a big one, and they put it in his cot under the blanket and he found it and they sat there and they were so disappointed when he just scooped it up and tossed it outside. So then late that morning they took him out to the latrine to talk and then they beat the hell out of him and he didn't do anything.

He stopped and contemplated his cup of tea. He smiled as much to himself as to anything else and then he put the cup down on the table between us. The tea smelled of lemon and mint. I smelled the mint strongly and the scent of pine that came from the trees.

—I was sick then. I had the runs so bad, I couldn't do anything. After a few days it started to go away and we got the word to move and we were taking everything down and we were all set to go and the kid was the last one and everyone was yelling at him to hurry up and we're sitting on the carrier, I don't know what you call it in English, but we're on it and he's walking slowly towards us and he drops his bag in the middle of the field and everyone's yelling and he's really calm, even smiling, and he stands there, takes his gun. Cocks it, lowers it so the barrel is against his neck and pulls the trigger, just like that. There was such a tremendous spray of blood and I remember a piece of the back of his head going up and turning in a circle with blood coming off it like a Ferris wheel lit up for a carnival, spinning and turning until it fell down to the mud.

I didn't say anything. There didn't seem to be anything to say that I knew that would have mattered.

—The thing is, he said, you have to go. You don't go you're an idiot. But it doesn't matter.

—Why?

—Because the same story will catch you in another place only the costumes and the accents will be different and the themes will be local but universal too. It's a trap. Existence is a trap.

—Yes.

—A beautiful girl asks you to meet her anywhere, but in West Berlin, in the winter and you've already been with her so that's already happening and the ministry thinks you're a punk, you have to go, but there's another thing.

—What's that?

—If you go, he said solemnly, it will ruin you for a normal life.

He stared at me very intently, and then he started to laugh and he kept laughing and soon I was laughing too and we sat there laughing until we stopped and he said, riders on the storm, and we drank our tea and were quiet and then after a while I said goodnight, and walked home and thought about the great shower of blood and I did not want to laugh about anything and I lay in bed and stared at the ceiling and felt empty and full at the same time, but like a weight that was stuck from being too heavy to move and then all at once, I snapped out of what had been a half-dream of someone knocking at a door and looked out the window. There was a thin streak of bruised sky lit up deep-blue-black with the rising sun and I watched it grow.

ᘛᘚ

Faulkner's Sparrows

An Interlude in the form of a Brief Essay

At the beginning of William Faulkner's Absalom! Absalom! we are told that the sparrows were coming and going in a random gust. I have found this an oddly mysterious and perplexing statement.

There are two competing ideas at work in the gesture of the sparrows' movement. The first is that, Faulkner is correct and that the birds, without purpose in their movement, drift for no reason other than in response to random stimuli which cause them to go from one place to another. The second is that there *is* a reason and either Faulkner did not perceive it or did but chose instead to describe the movement of the sparrows as a sign of drift reinforcing the drift of the burdensome heat and the weight of time both present and absent and contained in memory and memory itself reflecting time and the idea that time being both now and past is never what it appears to be but rather a river of interactive stimuli and response moving forwards and back and in circles at random like sparrows and twice-blooming wisteria.

I have been unable to penetrate to the truth of this but come down on the side of Faulkner making a choice to ignore what he must have known, which is that birds respond to scent and movement and that wind and scent and response are not random but rather manifestations of a sublime order often dimly perceived.

Yet, what if he was wrong and made a mistake and he was drunk or hung-over and he knew he was wrong but thought about it and decided it sounded good and reworking it would have slowed him down too much?

☙❧

For several years I found myself unable to reconcile Darwin and Freud. I had reached a point where I could find no reason, biologically, in a Darwinian sense, for the existence of insanity and its persistence in human events and its constancy in human action. The obvious answer would be, in a Darwinian sense, that abnormal behavior ultimately cancels out reproduction and such strands of DNA are in the process of being selected against or, they shall predominate and the species will die out. But, what troubled me was the constancy over time of irrational and counter-productive action that results in reproduction of strands of DNA that pose a clear threat to themselves and the survival of the species. If neuroses is a common condition and one of enduring normalcy (as Montaigne puts it, men are naturally insane, so to not be insane amounts to another form of insanity) then either Darwin is wrong, which I don't believe, or Psychoanalysis is wrong and insanity, *à la* Foucault is a fabrication, an adjustment for the purposes of power to the vast tide of interconnected pulses—economic-class-genetics-biology-psychology, *et cetera*.

To approach this from another angle: Why would nature bother, in its evolutionary method, to create a one-off strand of DNA that not only has the capacity to eradicate itself, and the rest of life, but a continuing habit of attempting to do just that? In other words, what evolutionary purpose does "insanity" serve if it has the habit of bringing its host to the brink of extinction, if as a potential spur to adaptation it is counterproductive because of the amount of damage it causes.

A zebra develops camouflage to give it an edge against lions and lions adapt by developing through violent methods of reproduction a higher yield of muscle and scent in a strand of increasingly superior cats (or a continuity of cats that are good enough to catch zebras and do not need to evolve and produce cars with which they would then chase all zebras to extinction) but there is an essential equilibrium at work in that the lions have yet to develop the habit of eradicating themselves in their pursuit of zebras and the zebras have yet to adapt by developing guided missiles. Thus, why is there only one species that has produced the ability to commit and have the habit of self-destruction and having done so, what purpose does it serve if we assume there is an evolutionary drive behind the process of adaptation?

ଷ ଷ

In his book, The Origin of Consciousness in the Breakdown of the Bicameral Mind, Julian Jaynes suggests that the great leap, the moment of individuation that has seemingly propelled humanity into its present state of self-awareness (the emergence of the "I") was the result of the development and evolutionary adaptation of the corpus callosum—the mass that connects the two cerebral hemispheres, and that prior to this, when one half of the brain "thought" the other perceived it as an external voice of command and authority—the voice of god and thus, god's "disappearance" from the later stages of the Old Testament correspond to the evolutionary leap forward in which god is brought within the conjoined hemispheres and becomes "I".

At one point, Jaynes discusses the advent of language some time immediately after or close upon the end of the last Ice Age. In passing, he mentions a particular quality of this phase—the Halo-Centric Thermal Maximum—the point at which the earth's orbit brought it again closer to the sun causing the ice to begin to melt. In this period, which occurred over several centuries, Jaynes mentions that it must have rained for something like three centuries and that it was after this that speech appears and humans begin to record themselves as being recorded self-reflexively through the agency of words that are themselves mirrors of words reflecting the human minds reflecting in and upon its own existence.

Within this though, is another issue that has received less attention than it might deserve. It is well documented and there is a vast corpus concerning the emergence at this time—circa 9-13,000 BC—of totemic figures depicting female forms holding shafts of wheat and barley; and this is added to the growing archeological record that has revealed ossified remains of wheat and barley and other bread-stuff that were gathered and consumed.

Reading Jaynes I thought about this, and Faulkner's sparrows and Darwin *contra* Freud and the following occurred to me: After three hundred years of rain, barley was bountiful and, being highly susceptible to ergot, became thick with ergot to the point of being a platform for a supra-form of the toxin, and that when consumed, attached itself to the new host; the human brain and there, between what became Broccas and Wernekes' Area, ergot became a mutation upon the DNA of the human form and created the illusion of "I" and came to be passed on both through the consumption of barley and through reproduction and as a result, the adaptation of speech and consciousness is an evolutionary mistake—not the great leap forward but, at best a giant step to one side, and at worst, a leap backwards; an evolutionary mal-adaptation leading inexorably to extinction.

ᘒᘒ

Why women? Why female figures holding wheat and barley? Because the men were hunting animals and the women were gathering food close-at-hand. But more still, the dark heart of the matter and the emergence of tropes of fearing and hating and worshipping women.

Hera, mother-goddess of the past has a name that means: throttle… to choke, or strangle. Why? Her totemic animal par-excellence is the sphinx who of course, asks three questions and if the challenger cannot answer them, is choked to death.

Why three questions? The answer of course is contained in the form of the riddle – what walks on four legs in the morning, two in the afternoon and three at night... man... the child becomes the man who becomes the old man who dies... three corresponding to the sequence of the tripartite biology of gestation... nine months... divided into three periods of three—three becoming one of a series of magic totemic numbers used repeatedly in stories that reflected the experience of living in a world ordered precisely as a vast mechanism that can be mapped with numbers as if math were a proto-genome project.

But why choke? Why so many snakes in and with women? Medusa, and Eve and cults of snakes and Apollo strangling the python...

Because umbilical strangulation utterly confounded and traumatized the ancient mind. Women contained snakes. Women were snakes. Failing to observe rituals could and often led to the turning into stone (still-born or stone cold dead on arrival) of newborns who died for the original sin that predated their birth and was committed by the parents who had violated a taboo which, à *priori*, must have been committed because the strangulation would not have occurred if the rituals had been properly observed to begin with.

Thus, the very earth was itself a fulcrum of incestuous interwoven catechisms that could not be avoided but were often violated resulting in necessary catastrophes.

So, ergot in barley and women with snakes and hallucinations and the voices of gods and demons and the rise of cults and the shock-trauma of umbilical strangulation and a miasma of word-consciousness and cults dedicated to barley because barley and women and birth and death and sex did not come and go in random gusts but came and went with design and precision and the great flaw in the design is manifest in consciousness which is a sterling example of evolution and evolution produces that which works and that which fails and in failure dies out, choked off into evolutionary oblivion, unless it adapts, unless it transforms, unless it is a bad design to begin with.

ᛝ ᛢ

The Sword in the Stone & Raymond Chandler

The waitress in the story said her name was Dottie. She showed me her name tag to emphasize the point. It said: Hello My Name is Dottie.

I nodded and smiled with as much conviction as I could muster. I was not convinced that Dottie was impressed with my sincerity. I thought Dottie believed I was a worthless illusion.

I told Dottie what I wanted. She said she would be right back with my order. She poured me a cup of coffee before she left.

I enjoyed the view of the freeway while she was gone, and then turned from the big window to enjoy the view of the obese trucker sitting across from me. I stared at him until he looked at me with his big porcine face and as he seemed to be in agreement with Dottie regarding my moral failing, I went back to looking at the freeway.

I stared at the freeway. I counted cars. I counted small cars and big cars, red cars, blue cars and cars with bumper stickers. I counted SUVs. I wondered how many marines to the gallon they got.

Dottie returned with my food. She looked at me with a fair amount of disappointment and left the check on the table. In her eyes, it was three in the morning on a Tuesday.

Then somewhere far away that looked like La Jolla on a warm rainy day, Raymond Chandler began to contemplate a bottle of gin. It is impossible to explain this directly. But there it is. Or perhaps it is best to say it is an elaborate metaphor.

Regardless, this is what happened. His phone rang. He let it ring three times. He was wearing white gloves a blue robe and a pair of blue pajamas and brown leather slippers. On the other end of the phone a man was standing in a small metal tub of cold water. He was wearing a blue suit. His pants legs were rolled to his knees.

He said: My name is Mr. White. The Ministry sends its regards.

Then he hung up the phone. Raymond put the phone down and he returned to contemplating his bottle of gin. He was weighing the merits of straight gin versus gin with tonic. Then it started to rain harder than before and the rain sounded sharp against the roof. Soon it was raining so hard and the wind was blowing with such force and it was so warm, that Raymond began to think he was in a monsoon.

He wondered if you could have a monsoon in La Jolla or even a place that looked like La Jolla but was somewhere else instead.

He thought about the call. He thought it was a prank. He thought about people he knew at the studio. The wind blew and the rain fell like a fat angry drunk sliding off the end of a cheap bar.

Raymond thought about a gin and tonic. It was humid outside and he thought about the east. Monsoons were in the east. Asia had monsoons. Gin and tonic was a British drink. It was an imperial drink. Kipling should drink gin with tonic or without tonic. Here's to Kipling thought Raymond. Then he thought gin and tonic and monsoons were a cliché.

He wanted to avoid clichés.

He thought about a rum punch. He decided it was rum punch weather. It was imperial monsoon weather. He decided to go downstairs to the bar. He got dressed. He traded his pajamas for a lightweight tan suit a white shirt and a blue and gold striped tie and a pair of loafers with tassels. He kept the gloves.

He took the elevator down to the lobby and from the lobby he walked to the bar. The rain was still falling like the fat drunk and the wind was still blowing and as he walked to the bar, the wind increased and began to push the rain sideways in great thick sheets and Raymond was still thinking about a rum punch.

The bar was dark in the manner of American bars and there was a restaurant attached to it and the two were separated by a wall in which there was a small open square and the waiters and bartenders spoke to each other through it.

The bar was empty except for one bartender and then Raymond. Raymond pulled off his gloves and placed one on top of the other on top of the bar. The bartender said hello. She was not wearing a name tag. She asked if he wanted a gin and tonic. He said yes. At the last moment he changed his mind. He had thought rum punch but he changed his mind and said yes to the gin and tonic and then as he sat down the waitress leaned in through the open square in the wall and spoke to the bartender. She said: Do you know how to make a rum punch; this guy wants a rum punch.

The bartender said she did not know how to make one. They both looked at Raymond. He said he did not know either.

The waitress went away and the bartender made a gin and tonic and served it and Raymond sat there thinking about the phone call, the drink, and the man who ordered the rum punch. The rain came on strong with the wind blowing it sideways and it beat against the windows.

☙☙

Special Agent Automatic Turpentine

Special Agent Automatic Turpentine circles words in a book that are to be deleted before publication. He comes across a word that leaves him feeling unsure of what to do so he reaches for a volume of The Book of Regulations. He opens it and is shocked to see that the book has changed. He puts it back on the shelf. His hands are trembling. He is alone in the office yet he is afraid someone will see his trembling hands. He looks at the bookshelf. There are rows of big blue books. These are the books of the regulations, volume I-XVIII, with seven appendices.

He pulls volume III down from the shelf again. He

opens it. It does not contain the regulations. He puts it back on the shelf and pulls down volume VII. It too has changed. He hears people go by in the hallway outside of the office. He thrusts his hands into his pant pockets. He takes them out and looks at them as if they might belong to someone else. The voices in the hall fade and Special Agent Automatic Turpentine takes down volume IX. It no longer contains the regulations. He flips through the pages and finally stops and reads:

In the country of the novel the General with the head of a rabbit has a meeting with the Maximum Leader. They pose for photographs. They stand together in the middle of a dusty road somewhere in a mythical place called Texas.

The Maximum Leader is tired. He has not been sleeping well. His wife has been away on a goodwill trip and he has had trouble sleeping without her. He has had troubling recurring dreams.

In the dream, his wife is seventeen and he only knows her distantly. She lives in Texas. She is in love with a boy named Richard who everyone calls Buck. Buck is—was—the quarterback of the local high school football team.

This is true, but it is also true in the Maximum Leader's dream so it is false and true and both and neither or perhaps, truly-false and falsely true. No matter. This is the dream of the Maximum Leader and it reoccurs every night.

In the narrative of the dream the Maximum Leader's wife is enraged because Richard, who everyone calls Buck, has left her for another girl. She, the girl who will become the empress, knows that Buck will be driving to see the girl at seven. She knows when he will leave his parent's house and how long it will take for him to arrive and she takes the keys to her father's car and drives with a precise clock ticking in her throat at the base of the almond colored bird that powers the exact and exacting mechanism of her brain, which is organized as a vast palace full of dutiful, servile attendants, who smile and bow and wipe puddles of piss and vomit from behind enormous vases in glittering halls. She arrives at the intersection of three roads and there will be no inquest, no report, only a vaguely worded statement by the responding police officer, who will find her sitting in her car, just sitting, and find Buck shot through the side window of his car—defenestrated—shred of clothes and most of his skin and so much blood, blood in pools and narrow expanding rivers gullies and streams and splashes thrown through the air making extravagant splashes on the dark pavement and the Maximum Leader inhales his Chappaquiddick (of which no one speaks) and lets out a blast of air that smells like an elephant at the moment of its death.

ॐ ॐ

The Maximum Leader's wife says her favorite piece of literature is The Grand Inquisitor. Because no one reads and because she is surrounded by functional illiterates and lackeys no one asks her about this. No one asks her if she believes god will be rejected by those who claim to serve god with devotion. No one asks her the meaning of faith or if she is insane or if she is consumed with guilt or if she feels nothing at all except the dead weight of years of repression and anti-depressants and no one asks her if she ever looks at her husband and thinks that in the absolute infinite reach of eternity she is certain god has abandoned them.

ॐ ॐ

The General sits in the Maximum Leader's living room. Heavy tooled leather furniture. A case with guns. A bronze statue of a man breaking a horse. Cups of coffee and a pitcher of mint tea for the General's delicate stomach. The details of empire.

—It's going well, the General says, except for the rain.

—Yes, says the Maximum Leader, that rain;

damndest thing. Whatd'ya say there Dick?

Dick crosses one leg over the other. He has a solid indoor tan.

—Damndest thing sir, but General, I assure you, we've got the best people working on it, the best. We're going to get some things on television; we've cracked their code and we're going to get some shows on the television. There's one about these rich kids full of dialogue that contains the code you know hip slang that people use and another about a math genius who helps his brother who works for the Ministry. It's a high-tech dragnet. Hip, very hip.

—The rain, says the General, looking at Dick, while his big fluffy ears tilted a little, has seeped into everything. My wife is wearing red. A statement to lift people's spirits, if you take my meaning.

The Maximum Leader nods his head.

—A statement, that's the thing we need. Turn this rain thing into a positive.

—A positive, says Dick, yes sir, a positive. The television idea; it's a positive.

The General nods his head and strokes his long white whiskers. He wrinkles his big pink nose. He thinks the Maximum Leader smells like an elephant at the moment of its death.

✄ ✄

Special Agent Automatic Turpentine closes the Book of Regulations. He is dripping with sweat. The sweat stings his eyes. He smells his sweat. His face is damp. His fingernails are tinted with sweaty lines of red. He feels the tension of his bladder filling with urine. He is not sure why but he smells bread. People walk by in the hall outside of his office.

He waits for them to pass by and then, quietly, he goes to the door and reaches to turn the knob, but his palms and his fingers are slick and he must grab the knob with his jacket, and he turns it; opens the door, and walks quickly to the nearest men's room and there, he washes his hands.

He speaks to no one about what has happened; what he has read. He goes outside and walks around the building. He stops near the entrance to the metro. He stands and stares. He looks at the people passing on the sidewalk, the cars drifting by; the light poles. He stares at a parked car.

He reads the license plate. It says: *pet girls*.

A man passes close by him. Their eyes meet and exchange the greetings common to eyes meeting for the first and one-hundredth time. The woman in the car watches them pass each other and she thinks: paranoid and on the edge. From above, rain turning slowly to snow, begins to fall.

☒☒

Tiresias in Love

"I regret to say that we of the FBI are powerless to act in cases of oral-genital intimacy, unless it has in some way obstructed interstate commerce."

— J. Edgar Hoover

ᘒᘒ

The Battle for Café Algiers

I saw her through the window. She was with two men. They were with her. I didn't know them. One was a tall thin man, in blue leather pants. The other was smaller and had long hair tied in a ponytail. He was leaning across the table running his hands over a bottle of beer. In his face, it was clear, that he was with her, even if she was not really with him.

I looked at her. I looked at her through the window. She was smoking. I saw her mouth moving and her hands going but I couldn't hear her. The window slid back and forth on thin metal rails but it was closed then, so I just stood there watching her. She always spoke with her hands going, flying them through the air like small dark birds that did not know their way home. Or, perhaps it was that she flew them through the air like small dark homes that did not ever know the shape of a bird. I can't say. And, even if I could,

I'd keep it to myself.

Leather pants stood up and floated towards the bathroom. His pants hung low on his narrow waist and he walked with his hands held out in front of him like magnets pulling his body softly, in another direction.

A young boy with something shiny on his lips, walked passed me. He smiled, shyly. I looked away and he passed on, slowly filtering into the knot of people standing on the corner.

I looked at Adiah. She made me feel hungry. I looked at the other man. I'd seen him before coming out of the bookstore. He was staring hard at her. I knew the look. People looked at her that way all the time, as if they were hungry or thirsty but hadn't known it until that moment. It hurt them a little, but then, it wasn't a terrible thing to know, watching her lean forward over the table. She said something to him. He laughed. He laughed, but he was laughing too much. She wasn't that funny. She was never that funny. I knew it, but I smiled all the same because I liked watching her with him.

I felt a kind of nausea at the sight of it at first, of her with him, but then it was a pleasant feeling of knowing a secret, of knowing something no one else knew, and knowing it with absolutely no regrets.

She leaned forward again, her face going behind the big green block letters that spelled out the name of the café. I stood there, leaning against a lamp post. She leaned back and her lovely brown face appeared behind the letters. She saw me. She stood up and went to the door.

She came outside, her hair, seaweed tendrils, the sound of the café coming with her through the door as she opened it, going away as the door closed behind her.

I saw leather pants come back, the other one, ignoring him, watching me instead.

—Hello Jake, she said, winking, and laughing, you got my message.

—I got it, I said, ignoring her joke; that's it.

—Don't play the character, she said, smiling, shrugging her shoulders.

—You seem all right, I said, pointing vaguely with my chin, at the café.

A car went by, blaring music with a heavy bass-beat. It made the air rattle. It passed through me. The car was painted with racing stripes and logos. On the side it said: *Club Paradoxa*.

She dropped her cigarette on the sidewalk. She stepped on it. She was wearing a blue tee-shirt, jeans, and high-tops. Her hair was uncombed, as always. She thrust her hands into her pants and looked at me. On her shirt it said: *The Whips london is unavailable*.

—His name's Daniel, she said; he's from Cleveland.

—And leather pants, I said, watching a large woman walk past us, staring at Adiah.

—His name's Peter, she said; he's from Hamburg, I think. Or maybe, London. He likes Jewish boys. Says he finds them exotic. But mostly, he's terribly in love with a boy named George.

—Is that right? I said.

—No one's asking for your permission, she said, pulling her hands free.

—Now what? I said.

—I'm going to have another beer. You with us?

—I'm tired, I said. I should be writing.

She didn't answer. I looked up the street. A crowd was spilling out of Shunra, the pub on the other corner. The traffic was getting tighter in the narrow streets. Over the high wall of the compound I could see the flag, hanging like a limp idea in the heat. The air smelled faintly of car exhaust. I looked back at her.

—I think I'll go home, I said, seeing the flecks of paint on her wrists. They looked like tattoos.

—Don't pout, she said, I hate it. It's not that terrible, really. Besides, we could talk about things. You can belong if you want to.

—What's he want? I said.

—Him? She said, looking from me to the café and back again. I told you.

—I meant Cleveland.

—Oh, she said, *him*. He thinks if he gives me a pot plant, I'll go to bed with him. You know, if property is theft, gifts are bribery. Sex is currency.

I didn't say anything. She looked at me with something that crossed disappointment with hurt and I felt like melting. A truck went down the street, slowly turning at the corner. Across the back was a sign for Pul-man cigarettes. There was a bright image below the logo of a man resting by a large rock at the base of a steep hill. There was a caption. It said: *everyone deserves a break*.

She stepped close to me. I was looking at her eyes. She raised herself and kissed me. Her hands brushed me. Her tongue came into my mouth and we had our lips wet together, touching her mouth full of the dry beer-scent and the taste of smoke. Then she stepped away. I watched her going. It was like a bright light had gone on, then off and I watched her.

—That, she said, will kill him.

—Is that why you did it? I said.

—I did it, she said, because I wanted to do it, and you know that. The rest is just how it reads.

The large woman had come back and was stepping behind Adiah. A crowd of people passed in-between us and the large woman opened the door. She held the door, then went inside when she saw Adiah standing there, looking at me. The crowd passed, then she smiled at me.

—I can come later, she said.

I didn't say anything. We stared at each other.

—Do you want me to come later? She said.

—I'll be at home, I said, so, you can come, if you want. But I won't stay up.

That stung her. Maybe I meant it. She smiled but it didn't reach her eyes. Her eyes were hard, big, brown, wet almonds in her narrow, dark face. She was hurt, then angry. Then, the smile left and I watched it slip up into her eyes, going quickly away from her mouth. I was forgiven and we both knew it. She stood there a little longer, the noise spilling out around her.

She went inside and leather pants and Cleveland watched her. I watched too. I watched her walk across the café. She was walking where the letters were on the window. Her head seemed separated from her body by the letters. I watched her, then, I turned and walked back the way I had come, walking all the way home.

I waited for her. I waited for her and stayed up waiting, even though I said I wouldn't. I always waited for her. She knew it. Alone in the gathering dark, I kept thinking about her, waiting, saying her name again, and again, and again, a magical incantation that brought me nothing. Then, I fell asleep, waiting.

ﻭﻭ

Later I heard someone knocking on the door. I got up, put on my shorts and went to the hall. I said, yes, and I heard her. I went to the door and Adiah was there.

—Can I come in? She said.

I didn't say anything. I stepped aside and opened the door as wide as I could and she came in and shuffled down the hall. I closed the door and followed her.

She stopped in the middle of the room, turned and I stood there, looking at her. She walked to me and I put my arms around her and we kissed. I kissed her, and everything began again.

∅ ∅

Baltimore

In the photograph, Samantha is turning and looking back at me as she goes down the alley to the hotel. It is winter. My birthday. She has taken us to Baltimore for the weekend and when she asks, in the room, if it's good, I tell her truthfully, it's the best it's ever been, a birthday worth remembering and she shows me the truth in her soft brown eyes and she does not ask after Audrey or Berlin or Adiah and we were alone together and looking out the window over the balcony we watched the snow come and there were no spies and outside the wind pushed the snow and then snow became rain and we listened to it beat against the windows and the rain said sleep and we did.

☒ ☒

In our dream the library is forever and delicate

"Your last letter left me in a fine mood. I celebrated by having a cup of orange tea in the garden beside the olive tree. In our dream the library is forever and delicate and it is the record of what can be imagined and there is no last answer and no beginning and each one who enters finds the story they need...and in the end they can listen and go on listening; Aleous I pity. "

— Lesharc A. Koffkalt

— Letters to Cavafy

☒ ☒

The Drift

I can find no reason for anything and everything seems to be a reason for itself and we drift and then there is the war and the war comes and goes and I see a man with a prosthetic leg that looks like an

131

elegant piece of sculpture and it curves and gives him the look of a man who has been blended with a chair from a store that sells Modern Danish furniture and I mention that to Samantha one evening over dinner in a restaurant and a week later on a television show about a federal cop who helps people into a witness relocation program, there is a man who has a prosthetic leg and the cop says what she says about Danish Modern and the show is full of clever pop culture references and it is well reviewed and I drift beyond rage or tears and I feel myself shut down like a television screen fading to a dull slate gray.

The Job

I had a job. I sat in a cubicle and made calls. I tried to convince people to let us write letters for them that said they were in favor of something happening near their home, except when I made calls to people and tried to convince them to let us write letters expressing how they were against something happening near their homes. We made many calls. We wrote many letters. We mailed them to people in the government. Things happened. Sometimes nothing happened.

John

John was the assistant manager and he was the one who told me the bosses were concerned about Mike. He said they wanted him to say something to Mike, about how he smells and he whispers this to me while we're standing by his desk. Phones are ringing. You can hear a few voices soft and kind of hollow. The florescent lights are dull and the gray carpet is dull and there's the dull white of the adjustable cubicle walls; it's like living inside a factory where there's only ever been one idea and the place feels sterile, quiet and efficient, and it's true Mike weighs near three hundred pounds and he smells sour like really old apples and he didn't smell efficient at all even though he was and was good at the job and kept the sales department afloat and made the bosses look good.

I said, Well what are you going to say? and he said, I asked them if I could bring you in on this and I said, What do you want me to say? You smell bad, you need to lose a hundred pounds and by the way people are talking about how you make them gag? and then he'll probably sue everyone for harassment or something and win and John got this very serious look as if he was suddenly inside the moment of his life breaking like a finger caught by a heavy door and he said forget about it I'll tell them to forget about it and that's what happened—they forgot about it and that was the job and I went back and forth on the train and the metro and there were cameras everywhere and no one said anything about it.

☙☞

"Is Your Washroom Breeding Bolsheviks?"

One day on the train a man sat next to me. He turned and looked at me.

—Work in the District, he said. It was not really a question.

—Yes, I said.

—Me too. I'm a lawyer, for an agency.

He paused. The train rolled and there was the sound of metal grinding and the frame of the car stretching, moaning and then the pounding beat of the wheels turning on the track.

—I handled an interesting case last week. An obese man sued a company for telling him he smelled bad. Imagine that.

He stared at me. He stared out the window. He turned and stared at the back of the seat in front of him. I looked out the window and watched the old small towns roll by and each one had once been a rail-stop and then they were just old small towns and there was a quarry where they broke up cement and another where they did something with old rusted sheets of metal. I leaned my head against the window and the vibration rattled my head and I heard a deep buzzing as if there were a hive in my head, but I kept my eyes closed and the buzzing took over my skull and it was the only sound and I could not conjure any words and I stayed like that the whole time and when we got to the station, the man next to me got up and went to the door and said nothing and did not look at me and I watched everyone get off the train and walk down the platform to the exit.

ØØ

Story No.7

John had a girlfriend he didn't want and his girlfriend went and got a girlfriend to make him happy. So he had his girlfriend while she had her girlfriend and he never touched his girlfriend's girlfriend but only watched and that made him happy for a while to enjoy one with great feathery wings and the other who hummed like a vast neon sign and I started calling him Caligula and that was kind of funny except for when it wasn't.

So we'd sit for a little while at his desk in the office or go downstairs to the generic café in the building and get coffee. There was a view of the river slate grey and silent and he'd tell me about his weekends with the girlfriend and her girlfriend who it turned out had a boyfriend which as you'd expect didn't disrupt anything or anyone and I did not tell him anything and I hid myself and the truth and that went on for a while until his girlfriend said she had gained too much weight. She said she didn't feel sexy anymore and she wasn't sure if she should take the job in Boston or not and he said I just have no idea what I think about anything and we watched the coal train pull out of the yard down by the river.

Alisa

I met her in Old Town. She was waiting tables in a restaurant and she said she was from Romania and the things you noticed right off were that she was six feet tall, thin and beautiful. Her accent was thick but she spoke English well enough and when I asked her to pose for photos, she said yes and shrugged her broad shoulders with the practiced disdain of a woman who'd spent years defying attempts to be purchased, and she made it clear one evening as I was taking photos of her for a man named Hassan who ran a boutique on King Street. We had gone out to the alley behind the shop. It was winter and she was wearing heels, tuxedo pants and a man's white shirt with a thick blue tie, stunning, sexy, impossible, all of it impossible. She looked down at me and smiled saying no one can buy me; she said I go when I want, I come when I want, you understand, and from inside her hands hulking farm boys smelling like bruised and bitter apples crawled out of broken crates in the woods of Romania and stood around her with thin hungry lips shaking their erect cocks at her. So I took the photos and we walked back to the store and I came just about up to her shoulder and it was very cold and our breath came in thick plumes like cat tails waving in the dark.

☒☒

I went back to the restaurant to show her the photographs. She wasn't there. I asked the bartender.

—Who?

—Alisa?

He stared at me.

—Six feet tall, I said. Accent. Legs for miles.

He stared at me and then the manager came over and asked if there was a problem. I said I was looking for Alisa. He stared at me.

—Gone.

—Gone?

—Yeah. Back to Romania.

—Just like that?

—Yeah, he said, just like that.

☙☞

Copies of Forgeries

"Estimates vary as to the total number of forgeries held in museums and identified as authentic works of art. This odd untruth attached as a strange spandrel to contemporary reality operates as a vast turn of the screw to ideas about culture and the co-modification of culture. The corollary is the question—to what extent has the notion of identity been transformed into a fiction with its uses stretched and contorted for various purposes in a kind of oblique act of self colonization in which after the body has been deconstructed into space-for-rent and whole-sale, what remains is the identity and the identity becomes an endless mirror repeating echoes of its previous falsehoods until the dialectic of lie in answer to lie assumes the power of a catechism thus rendering all attempts at order/identity false, thus creating the most obvious and successful of mass conspiracies—the idea of the individual; the idea of the free individual."

—The Rape of the Sabine

—Thomas P. Tanasky

ॐ

At the Hotel Morgan

In the television show based upon the novel, he met her poolside at the Hotel Morgan. She was there when he arrived. She was alone and sitting at a table smoking a cigarette. She smiled brightly as he came through the doors from the bar to the pool.

It was warm and the breeze was light pushing the surface of the water so that small blue waves snapped the tiles softly and you heard it as if someone was clapping gently.

—Ms. Peppe, said Raymond.

—Call me Utta, she said and gestured for him to sit.

A waiter in a tight white jacket appeared as if he had been waiting his entire life to appear at the side of the table and be told what to do next. They ordered drinks and the waiter went to get them.

While they waited she told him about her vacation plans. She was going to Paris to meet a friend. She spoke euphemistically about him and then she said she was meeting her other friends at a resort in Turkey. The waiter brought their drinks. The lights along the pool came on. They were deeply green and red and the water changed from blue to a deep shade of burgundy.

—Of course I've misplaced my ticket, she said and laughed the way wealthy people do when they were being forgetful about things other people took as seriously as death.

—I'm sure you'll find it; besides there must be a copy.

—Of course you're correct Raymond.

—So, what is it you wanted to tell me?

—Well, it is difficult.

He smiled warmly. She took a long swallow from her glass. The wind picked up and the water in the pool snapped against the tiles.

—Since my stepfather has retired, and has been living here, he has become, forgetful. It's a problem.

—For whom?

—Oh Raymond, you are so charming. I was speaking to Mr. White about you. Have you spoken with him? He's one of my stepfather's oldest friends.

Ray looked at her. She was smiling but her eyes were flat and he thought about her losing the ticket and he thought about a fashion magazine he'd seen in the office of his doctor. It was funny that way; things colliding in the space between one thought and another and he thought about the photograph of the two heiresses; twins.

—The General did not mention him.

—Oh, she said, I should give you his information. He could be very helpful.

—With?

—Now Raymond, don't be difficult, we're getting along so well, and you know I only want to help.

—With?

She laughed and leaned back in her chair. She crossed one long leg over the other so he could see them. They were long and lovely and she knew it and he did too.

—My stepfather is getting old, she said, and that list of names–he should have burned it years ago.

Ray stared at her. He smiled warmly again. She stared at him and then she smiled and reached into her purse. It was a small elegant black bag with a small gold plate near the drawstrings.

In the story as it is told, the moment where history has its revenge is now. It is simple and almost funny because she is certain she is doing the right thing and in the story as it is told later, she places Mr. White's card on the table because she wants Ray to be afraid, to leave the list alone and to forget the name that has fallen from the ledger of time and she is polite and beautiful and leaves the card on the table saying she has to be going.

He stands when she stands and she kisses him on the cheek. She brushes close to him and he smells her perfume and she squeezes his arm with just enough pressure to suggest something vague and then she is gone and he thinks it is as if he were watching a regal yet glacial ballerina.

He sat at the table and worked on his drink. The water in the pool came and went in a steady back and forth and he watched the colors drift over the surface.

☒☒

In our own time, the analogy between war making and state making, on the one hand, and organized crime, on the other, is becoming tragically apt.

— Charles Tilly

☒☒

A Conversation

In the country of the novel the red stain continues to grow. It spills out of the room carrying Herr Metternich and the members of the junta. Herr Metternich is sitting in a great silver punch bowl. His eyes are big and he is calling for his security detail, but they have been swept down the street.

People stand in the streets. Everything is turning red. The streets are red and so are people's clothes and their skin. It begins to rain and the rain is red or perhaps it only seems red and the clouds are red as well and Herr Metternich is calling to the General –

The family jewels; I told you if they were released the streets would run red.

But the General does not answer. He is sitting atop an ornate globe spinning around and around, hurtling down the Grand Avenue of Winged Victory. People are watching him in disbelief. The General, they say, looking up from their red clothes and their red skin. It must be a sign of the apocalypse.

In his apartment, the author stands by a window and watches the streaks of red rain wash down the glass. He is listening to a Bach cello suite. It sounds he thinks, like the gears of creation, turning precisely. Then, there is a knock at his front door.

He goes to the door and has a premonition. He sees clearly in his mind who will be there when he opens the door. He opens the door and smiles.

It is as he thought, as he saw it—the lawyer from Madrid, dripping with red rain, his tan trench coat glowing damp and red under the soft light in the hallway. Above the lawyer from Madrid there is a skylight. The rain pours down on it and he looks up and then he looks back at the author.

—You know who I am? He says.

—Yes, says the author, I knew it was you.

—It was in your eyes; the look of recognition.

—Well, you're here. You might as well come in and begin.

The lawyer, who was named Pepe Guzman, took

off his wet coat and stepped into the foyer. Ariel, who was the author, took the coat and brought it to the bathroom and hung it on a hanger over the shower. He stood there for a moment and watched the water drip from the coat falling in small red drops that exploded and formed small crowns and then made tiny puddles in the basin. He watched the water run slowly towards the drain. He turned and walked into the living room and saw Guzman standing where he had stood, looking out the window.

He had set the stereo to repeat. The music, elegant and precise, beautifully sad and exultant as any act of creation, turned around and around in the old room and the rain came on steadily beating against the glass and Guzman, without turning, his voice bouncing off the glass and thus seeming to arrive twice, said,

—It's extraordinary, this rain, but I'm sure someone will explain it, they always manage to explain things.

Ariel did not say anything. He wanted to ask who 'they' were but he knew and said nothing. On his writing table a notepad lay open—exposed, he thought, as if it were a piece of dirty clothes or a woman, with her legs spread and they were standing there pretending not to notice when of course they did.

—So, said Guzman, the court has received files that make clear the ways in which the Ministry has drawn a net connecting people and how this information has been used for—he paused—illegitimate purposes.

Ariel stood watching Guzman watch the rain. His heart beat heavily and he felt a headache begin to step in time to his heart, the pain bouncing behind his right eye.

—Needless to say, said Guzman, your name has come up.

—Needless, said Ariel.

Guzman turned and stared at him. Ariel extended his hands to the couch and chairs. Guzman walked to the chair with its back to the window and sat down, crossing one leg over the other. He extended a hand towards Ariel as if he were being polite and at the same time, in command.

Ariel hesitated but then sat down across from him. The music stopped and then began again.

—This, said Guzman, is all very complicated.

—This?

—Yes, he said, it's as if the government has written an elaborate story and calls it fact, when, in truth, it is all a great fiction.

—How's that?

—Well, take the war, for example; invading Babylon to capture Gilgamesh. The white whale as it were, of the Ministry's fevered imagination.

—How do you mean?

—They make up a story to suit what they want to be true and then pursue it with a vengeance.

—Oh, said Ariel, you mean lies are made into a universal system.

Guzman smiled. He had a long face that went up from his long neck like a V and at the tip of his chin down to the point of a dark black goatee.

—I always found it to be an important book, badly written.

—Well, it might be the translation; as someone put it, reading a book in translation is like making love to a woman through a blanket.

—Quite.

—So.

—So, said Guzman, it's all going to come out. The Committee will have all of the documents in the end and there will be hearings.

—Conducted by the very people who looked the other way while the flood came.

—They will have the documents.

—And shall I receive a knife to my heart?

—Abraham and Isaac go to Prague. Well, probably not so dramatic. On the other hand everything you've done is based on theft, lies, and deception. Your play about Picasso.

—Have you spoken with C?

—Not yet.

—They'll probably kill him before you have a

chance.

—Perhaps. But then they will be investigated for that. So it doesn't matter.

—It might matter to him.

—Perhaps. But not to me; my interest is in the law.

—Lawyers make such good sociopaths.

—Yes.

—So.

—Well, said Guzman, why not start at the beginning?

—Shouldn't I have a lawyer and shouldn't someone be taking notes?

—This is an informal conversation. It is on my authority. Besides, we already have the verdict. The law works best backwards from the truth to what we want, not from what we want going forward towards the truth.

—One assumes it's the other way around.

—One would be wrong to do so.

—Well, would you like some tea, or coffee, or something to eat?

—No, thank you.

—Alright then. Do you always speak like this?

—How am I speaking?

—A strangely self-aware stiffness.

—As you say.

—So?

—You were arrested.

—Yes.

—Tell me about that.

—But you already know.

—Yes.

—Then why?

—It is part of the story.

— It seems silly.

—You were having an affair with Ms. Pepe.

—Yes.

—And the Ministry found this out, how?

—They listened to C. A tap on his phone. He mentioned me, my novel –

—About the widows and the bodies in the river and Gödel?

—Yes. So they placed a tap on my phone. They heard me talking to Ms. Pepe. They placed a tap on her phone. They heard her talk to people. They put taps on their phones. *Ad infinitum ad absurdum*.

—Including Senator Bullet.

—Yes.

—And you were giving money to Ms. Pepe.

—Of course, she was my mistress, it is what one does. Even though it was silly; really a game we played.

—In what sense?

—Well, she was wealthy. She had far more money than I do or will ever have. But she allowed me to pay for her.

—Yes. And then the Ministry...

—Arrested me and said that she had given the money to certain people who had committed various crimes, which they called acts of terror.

—So you cooperated instead of going to prison.

—Yes. They said they would do things to her unless I helped them. They threatened me but made it sound as if they were doing me a favor at the same time.

—And as part of your cooperation, you began impersonating C?

—Well, not exactly, rather I was fed his material by the ministry and told to use it.

—Where?

—Several places. Television, the play about Picasso, my university lectures. My novel. Even one that was written to be badly reviewed so as to preempt any criticism. They fabricated accusations of plagiarism to tangle people up in court. It went on for years. Then I was told to offer C a job. He refused. They insisted.

—And did you know they were scripting television shows?

—It came up tangentially. Some of the agents mentioned it. They said it was an elaborate—he stopped, waved a hand in the air and looked at the window and the rain coming down running down the glass in streaks of red—sting. They said they were confronting an elaborate literary system of codes.

—To catch?

He looked back at Guzman. He stared at him for a moment. He listened to the music and the rain on the glass.

—Terrorists.

—Not a group known for watching elaborately scripted television shows.

—No, but they thought that C. was a leader, a wise man, that's what they called him. Not a soldier but a motivator. An imagination that could jump across time as someone phrased it. But really he was just sitting at home smoking weed and fucking his girl. And they knew they were being listened to so they stared a pantomime; a play that went on and incorporated everything that happened. The irony being that the more he confounded them the more they wanted him to explain things to them.

—And this was their conclusion based on listening to him talk?

—Apparently, I gathered from snippets here and there; things the agents said and the questions they asked me. He knew he was being recorded and he started talking and—

—Created a story to suit what they heard.

—It's always that way, isn't it?

—I knew a man, said Guzman, suddenly and without preliminaries, who wanted to write a novel.

He worked on it every day. He had his life organized around writing. Every morning, he woke, made coffee, fed his cat, and started to write. This went on for a long time. When he wasn't writing he worked for a company in the Old Town of a city writing reports. The job mostly made him miserable but it paid the rent. One day, on his way to work, he passed a construction site. He said excuse me to a man who was blocking his way and the man stepped to the side to let him go by and at that moment a large metal beam came loose, fell to the ground and hit the man—

—Which man?

—The writer.

—And?

—He died on the spot. Crushed. And a splash of blood, his blood, hit the other man right in the face.

—And then?

—Then, nothing, the writer, he was dead, end of the story until the law firm I worked for then had to interview people about the accident, for insurance purposes.

—Of course.

—Yes, so I interviewed the man who had stepped aside. He was a worker at the site. He had spent his life doing this kind of work, he got up every morning, had his coffee and went to a construction site and worked. Then, in the interview, he said it made him think about things, about god. That's what he said. I of course, paid no attention to any of it. I conducted the interview and told him that was that. But then, nine months later, it turns out there had been a mistake in the paperwork—a typo that led to the wrong man being accused of insurance fraud, and I had to interview him again. But the company said he had disappeared. Gone, just like that—one day he was gone. So, our firm hired an investigator to find him. And you know I have an appreciation for the work that investigators do. It's spade work, of course, but it must be done.

We found him eventually. He was in a monastery in the hills near El Corazon. I went there. I had to take a donkey up a narrow path. The donkey smelled badly, the dirt smelled just as badly; it was awful, the business of flies. I interviewed him in his monk's cell. He had found god, or rather, god had found him, and he said the accident had convinced him that he had to pray every night to ask for the faith to believe in god. Of course, he was crazy

—Crazy?

—Yes, said Guzman, mad. He asked me if I believed in god, and I laughed at him. He was shocked, looking at me with his sad, penitent eyes. I leaned across the little table there in his cell, with its one candle and one bowl, the props of his piety, and I said to him, my friend you are asking the wrong question. And he looked at me and was taken aback, and said, what other question is there of such importance other than that? And I said to him, I don't worry about my faith in god. No sir, what keeps me up nights is wondering if god believes in me.

They sat there staring at each other while the music played and the red rain continued to fall rolling down the window.

ɤ ȶ

Utta Pepe

Raven black hair up, exposing toffee colored skin and her neck exposed for his pleasure and her own. She places her overnight bag by the door—a change of clothes, a pair of jeans, sensible shoes and a pair that are not, a clean shirt, make-up, compact, phone, dildo with adjustable strap. She hears the voice of the concierge repeating 'I don't know' again and then heavy steps on the stairs, boots pounding. Later she will remember thinking about the third step before the landing, the step that always squeaked, and she will smile at noticing something so small so large so unimportant so vast. She hears them coming. She knows.

ɤ ȶ

Hassan Instructs

The boutique was elegant and the floor was polished marble. He sold shirts that cost three hundred dollars and suits for more than I made in two months. He liked to sit in the back and tell me about when he had been in law school in Florence.

He had one eye that drifted oddly as if it were looking for a way out from the rest of his head and he liked to talk about women.

Italian women, he said, were the best because they knew how to be with men. Then he laughed and said of course the men do not necessarily know how to be with women who know what they are doing.

—You, he said, should go to Italy. Every man should spend a year in Italy.

—I'm sure it's nice.

—You have to go soon though, he said and his eyes looked left and right.

—Of course, I said, soon.

He leaned close and whispered to me.

—It's the end of everything he said, and waved his hands in the air; do not be fooled. The end is coming and before it is all gone, you should go to Italy and fall in love twice.

—Twice?

—Yes, he said, twice. Once to do it and the

second time to always have something to remember when the end comes and then you can have one thing to keep to yourself after the last piece of your soul has been turned into a stock option.

Then he leaned back and he laughed. The phone rang and he stood and answered it, his voice bright and welcoming, and on the walls were the photos of Alisa.

⚲ ⚲

A More Perfect Union

"To be governed is to be watched, inspected, spied upon, directed, law-driven, numbered, regulated, enrolled, indoctrinated, preached at, controlled, checked, estimated, valued, censured, commanded, by creatures who have neither the right nor the wisdom nor the virtue to do so. To be governed is to be at every operation, at every transaction, noted, registered, counted, taxed, stamped, measured, numbered, assessed, licensed, authorized, admonished, prevented, forbidden, reformed, corrected, punished. It is, under pretext of public utility and in the name of the general interest, to be placed under contribution, drilled, fleeced, exploited, monopolized, extorted from, squeezed, hoaxed, robbed; then, at the slightest resistance, the first word of complaint, to be repressed, fined, vilified, harassed, hunted down, abused, clubbed,

disarmed, bound, choked, imprisoned, judged, condemned, shot, deported, sacrificed, sold, betrayed; and to crown all, mocked, ridiculed, derided, outraged, dishonored. That is government; that is its justice; that is its morality."

— Pierre-Joseph Proudhon

✆✇

How Does it Feel?

Once someone asked me what it was like, to be watched all the time and never know with any certainty if this was the moment when one of them might just slip their leash and push you in front of a bus, and you went swinging as a metronome from emptiness to fear and I said it was as if you were living behind your own eyes and every day you had to scrape away a little more of yourself with a rusty spoon and you were just waiting for the moment where you broke through and there was nothing on the other side and sometimes you laughed but then you remembered and you waited and then your phone would chirp or light up or someone would park in front of your apartment and sit there all night watching your door.

✆✇

The Farm

Special Agent Automatic Turpentine's parents owned a farm somewhere in Virginia. They bought a dog; a black Labrador puppy. One day, after the dog had grown older, it ran after the farm chickens and caught one and sank his teeth into it and blood sprayed in the air and formed dark patches on his muzzle and Turpentine's mother brought the dog to the barn and shot it and over dinner she said, to Automatic, If I tell you to train a dog, I expect you to train it.

☘ ☘

Alone

I live alone. I sleep alone. I have a cat. I had two cats, but one died. I wept for days when she died. Audrey went away and Samantha went away and I live alone. I lived alone when Audrey went away except for the two cats and every morning, when I got up to go to the bathroom and piss, the *Ministry* played a recording from a machine they had inserted into the floorboards of the apartment. It was the sound of a ball rolling across the floor. It was supposed to make me crazy but all it did was confirm to me that they were crazy. For a while they played the recording of a cat meowing but then they stopped. Above me was a woman who was a spy. One day I saw her lean out of her window wearing a tee-shirt that said: *San Marina County Sheriff* and later I ran into her in the foyer of the building and I said hello and she said hello and I said, excuse me but, are you a police officer and she froze and said, no… and did not say what she did, which is what people do when you ask and are wrong and she said nothing and then she walked away quickly and no one was there for me to say anything about it to and I thought, I should go to the bridge and jump and the aloneness has the weight of a vast body and it leans against you and nothing is there that you can point to, only the weight of it that you feel and no one believes you and the ones who do believe you are cowards so they lie and say they don't believe and then they run from you as if you were contagious, and the days become interchangeable and everything loses its flavor—texture becomes flat and the fingerprints of existence fade so that there is nothing unique and everything wears the gray costume of conformity and I watch television shows where the characters repeat what I had said to Audrey and I watch an interview with Ariel and he quotes me and the interviewer praises his book and in the country of the novel there is suddenly a shift in the narrative, yet a tone is maintained, and when asked the author says it is like jazz, like Coltrane, and they ask about the story within the within of the story within the novel and how the epic western the author writes is a timeless yet time-specific trope, the clarion call of the origin of the heart and blood of the junta, but he does not speak of the junta but only vaguely of a regime somewhere in a fictional country where it begins to rain and it does not stop and the rain is red, endless and red, falling through time and I sit there with the television on and the sound off and the cats asleep on the bed and I listen to myself breathing and the seconds that make the minutes that make the hours that make the day drip from my pores as blood that leaves no trace as if every fingerprint of existence has been erased, and I drifted alone up one street and then down the next and watched the bag people mumble the secret language of their visions and in the evenings I listened to my neighbor scream his way through his latest bout of delirium tremens and his name was Jack and he was a rail, nearly blind and an alcoholic and married to a woman named Alicia who was three hundred pounds plus a bagel. She ate and he drank, and then once every few months it wouldn't matter how much he drank because the hallucinations would start.

He said there were people coming out of the telephone and people in the hallways and I was alone and in the mornings there was the sound of the ball rolling and at night he would scream and once Alicia called the police and they took him away for a while and I saw her and she wept saying it was her fault buying him beer and vodka and she said if I don't he'll die and if I do he'll die and I stood there saying nothing, feeling only as if two enormous cold hands were pressing the sides of my head and the only people left to speak to were the ones who didn't care and the ones who were soon to be dead because they could no longer speak anything except the language of flies.

❧

If you dream of a jaguar, people are coming.
If the jaguar bites you, they are not people.
> —Eliot Weinberger
> —*Lacandons*

❧

A Theory of Entropy

In the film based upon the novel from the country of itself there is the story of the German girl with throat cancer who is rightfully accused of being an imposter, who hides her truth in order to protect her lover and every Sunday at three in the afternoon in the square in front of the church near the harbor, the local priest sits down in a chair, puts a revolver to the right of his head, presses the barrel against his skull, and plays Russian Roulette

✄ ✄

A crowd had gathered at edge of the square, filling it with heat and movement. They watched the priest. Some of them had made bets to see if this would be the day and others had made wagers saying it was not the day and still others prayed and someone said everyone is making a bet, it's just that some wager with money and the rest wager with their faith, but after a while no one said anything because everything had been said, every joke had been told, and there was the crowd and the priest with his gun. Some swore the priest recited a prayer before he pulled the trigger. Others disagreed. Some said the priest was a saint. An old man who had known him since they were both young said he had always been crazy. The first time was in the winter. It was raining. The rain came down straight as if from a vast shower and there was no wind, just the rain, and it made the sound of food on a hot surface sizzling and the priest had sat down on his chair in the square with his gun and a choir boy had come behind him and stood there holding an umbrella over him.

—It is absurd to be concerned with the rain, said the priest.

—It does not bother me, said the boy.

Then people began to notice. They asked if the priest was alright. Then someone (perhaps it was old man Shapinsky who was always noticing things) saw the gun. Soon, the chief of police came to see what was happening.

—Everything okay? he asked.

—Yes, said the priest, everything is fine.

—A lot of rain today, said the constable.

—Yes, said the priest.

—And the gun *padre*, what is the story with the gun?

—A matter between myself and god.

—I see, said the chief, and what would the gun have to do with that?

—I have decided, said the priest, raising the gun to his head, to resolve a question of faith.

Then, he pulled the trigger.

✄ ✂

"Film Lovers are Sick People"

In the film the German woman lies to protect the priest with whom she has had an affair. In the film this is presented starkly and many people are outraged and a story appears which shows a photograph of a woman wearing a black scarf and a reporter writers a story about a woman, the same woman in which it is revealed that during the war she had an affair with a priest and the priest shot himself and the woman was put on trial for a crime she did not commit but the court said privately though she may not be guilty of this, she is guilty of something and in the small town on the island she was sentenced and later her body washed up on the shore and it was as if many small fish had bitten her. Later when they were asked, the people of the town shrugged their shoulders as if to say fate is mysterious and no one knows anything.

ଙ଼ର

In the Hall of Mirrors

Freud is having coffee with Adler. They are at a café and they are drinking coffee and talking with strong vibrations suggestive of an underground stream full of jealousies and recriminations.

Adler speaks of his other café where he plays chess.

—Chess, says Freud, is interesting.

—Yes, says Adler turning to follow Freud's gaze.

Across the room there is a man with big eyes and he is writing in a small notebook and he looks up and stares at a regal woman with a glacial face and Adler thinks she looks exactly like a ballerina in a Russian ballet.

—So, says Adler, you know I've been treating this fellow for morphine addiction.

—The editor?

—Yes, well through him I've met one of his reporters. We've been playing chess. We take the children to the park.

—Yes.

—Yes, so this fellow... he's told me the most interesting screen memory. Very elaborate with just enough absurdity to be the truth. And he repeated something to me; an idea about a philosophy of the world.

—Yes.

—Well, so he is a committed revolutionary and says with complete conviction that he is going to overthrow the Czar. And he says, if the system is consistent it cannot be complete. And that, saying it is the nature of a system to be consistent and incomplete, is both true and not true at the same time.

—Continue.

—He is very intelligent but not afraid to use violence. Though his comments about philosophy are precise, like a Bach concerto mixed with a math formula or as if he were somehow drawing himself drawing himself. You know like Goya and the princesses.

—Yes. Obviously a system can be both complete and consistent.

—Yes, well the thing is… it's as if he's repeating lines from a script and I worked my way into challenging him on this. It took weeks for me to do it because he is so true to type; but once I did, it all happened very quickly. He broke down on the spot and told me the most amazing second screen memory. He told me that he is really an actor impersonating a real radical with whom he shares a physical similarity. He said the real radical had run off with an actress and he had taken the man's place. I stopped him and said, oh that's preposterous, right out of Conan-Doyle and Poe, the Scandal in Bohemia is the Purloined Letter, and he sank down further and he said to me that he swore it was the truth.

—Continue.

Outside a tram went by. They watched it and the sound of the wires popping in the misty air sounded like a cork being pulled and Adler turned and saw that the man who had been watching the woman who looked like a ballerina was gone. He took his pocket watch out and opened it.

—Well, said Adler, I am suddenly pressed for time; I seem to have lost fifty minutes from my watch. I apologize but if you will meet me this evening or here tomorrow I shall finish the story.

They agreed to meet the next day, at the same time. They passed the counter and Adler looked at a tin of chocolate.

—Droste?

—Yes, said Adler, I've developed an appreciation for it.

—Interesting.

—Yes, said Adler, the image on the cover makes me think of Giotto.

They stood at the counter and then the girl who had served them coffee asks if she could help them and Adler buys the tin and they go their separate ways.

$$\text{✄ ✄}$$

The Man from Hope

Once, he was very young and later, when he remembered being very young, he remembered watching his mother put on makeup. Later, he remembered that she went to work in New Orleans. He did not say what she did there exactly, but he knew. Later, the women in his life all resembled him, and he resembled his mother and all of his women wore a tremendous amount of makeup, except one of them who did not.

He nearly gave away the kingdom to the midgets who were trying to stage a *coup* but history had other ideas. We still liked him in spite of these things. We liked him and people asked how we could like such a son of a bitch, and we said, well yes, he is a son of a bitch, but he is our son of a bitch.

⚥

Czar of all the Russias

He was a major in a police station when the wall came down, and Germany was laughing. A crowd came to politely demand the keys to the kingdom and he strapped on a gun, grabbed a bigger gun, adjusted his uniform and went outside and like a cowboy on a dusty street in the middle of a nowhere town, stood defiantly before the crowd and calmly told them he would kill the first person who took one step closer. The crowd was a little tipsy on beer, mulled wine and success, but they got religion on the spot, and they decided to go ask for the keys to the kingdom from the cop down the road.

Later, when he was Czar, he held a ceremony for his coronation. He walked up a grand staircase. The stairs were marble and stretched all the way down to the basement like a great beard hanging from the face of an ossified saint named Basil or Sebastian and there was a red carpet on the stairs like the tongue of history, as if history might have a long red tongue, and he walked up the stairs and every few feet, men came to attention and they wore the uniform of 19th century cadets, because this was a dream and in the dream the old and the new were merged, as Napoleon had taken the crown from the Pope and placed it upon his own self and upon the self that was called Josephine, and the hammer symbolizes the city and the sickle symbolizes the fields of wheat as if to say the two are joined, but geography is a funny and mysterious thing and Moscow sits in the middle of nowhere like a great sun about which so many things go in orbit and one after another, the Czars come and the Czars go, saying in me here, what is in my left hand and what is in my right hand will be joined and in the great hall, he put one hand on a massive and ornate bible held by a spider disguised as a man who wore a great big black hat from which poured smoke and dusty dreams of the apocalypse and his other hand, he placed upon the flag and many people watched him and they were very proud, and when he came to France, Peter the Great saw many things—he saw high walls, and a mighty river, and he saw the king of France who had big bulging eyes and a great mustache and who said, 'I defeated the Dukes of Normandy with the will of god and canons supplied by the Turk', and

Peter turned, looked at himself repeated as if off an assembly line of History Incorporated reflected in a long hall of mirrors and at one end of the hall, he was very small, and at the other he was not so small, and he was Czar of all the Russias except one, which spun on the tip of one of his fingers, faster and faster, like a great and beautiful egg, and then it opened, and inside a small figure depicting a woman moved forward, and she spun in a circle, and a tiny bird, pecked at her outstretched hand, and time was in the egg, and it swept away everything except itself.

☙❧

Fishing in Cuba

Che sits below deck reading a book. Castro is on the dock talking to Hemingway about a fish. It is a big fish. A man takes a photograph. The three of them are in front of a crowd. Castro, Hemingway and the fish. They all have sharply focused eyes.

☙❧

'Listen to me,' says Castro chuffing the smoke of a cigar into the dark. 'I'm telling you I heard this straight from Khrushchev himself who got it straight from Stalin. Trotsky was not really Trotsky. He was an actor who played Trotsky for thirty years,' and Hemingway looks at Castro and says 'Brother, you're shitting me and I've been shat by the best. It's a con,' and Castro laughs and the Sierra Maestra shakes, the guards shift nervously from boot to boot and Hemingway drinks more rum and smokes more cigar and Castro says, 'I'm telling you, one night Stalin got tanked, completely bombed and he spilled the whole thing, the whole story,' and years later Khrushchev and Castro were wrestling in the winter trying to put snow down each other's pants and after he told him the whole story, how Trotsky had escaped prison in 1906 and was holed up for a night in this nowhere town in butt-fuck Siberia waiting for a sleigh ride back to St. Petersburg and the cops are on his tail and this theater troupe comes to the village that same night riding in on a big wagon and one beat up old Model T to put on a play—Chekhov's The Seagull, or maybe The Cherry Orchard, or some stray scenes from Hamlet—and Trotsky meets the lead actress and they fall for each other on the spot like a train wreck, a beautiful train wreck, and she tries to convince him to join the troop, but he says he can't, he believes in the revolution; and he tries to convince her to come with him, but she says she can't because she believes in the theater and there's this actor—the lead, who's in love with the girl, and he knows she doesn't want him as this has been going on for a year and three days of him writing her poems and she refusing, he singing her songs and she refusing, he cooking her a meal with food he's stolen and won by betting on a horse and she refusing, until eventually they all collide in the town, millions of particles and many hats and shoes and ideas all colliding in an elaborate pattern about which people say all sorts of things that are themselves echoes of the thing they are describing and he says to her, I love you this much— and this guy convinces Trotsky to join the troop in his place because this actor looks just like Lev and they switch places because this guy believes in love and Trotsky realizes he believes in the girl, and so the actor makes the contact and takes off with the cops chasing him and then thirty years later, whack in the head with the axe or ice-pick or whatever and Castro tells him how Khrushchev told him that Stalin only found out later and went crazy trying to find the real Trotsky and it gave him such stress that he had a heart attack because he couldn't tell anyone they'd killed the wrong guy and on his deathbed his last words were—Trotsky lives and I... — 'and that was it, he was gone, the dialectic of the absurd', Castro concludes and stops and smokes and smiles. Hemingway smokes, drinks, belches with profound gusto and they stare at each other with serious eyes that have seen many things too horrible to name and too funny for words, and then they laugh and

Hemingway says 'It's a hell of a story. Be better if it was true, but brother, take it from a master of the con, that story is bull', and Castro places his left hand on Hemingway's right shoulder and says, 'Brother, I shat you not. It's the truth, I swear to god', and the leaves of the banana trees shift in the light breeze and the guards shift in the light breeze and history sits on the tip of Castro's cigar and the tip glows red and turns grey.

⌀ ⌀

So Hemingway is sitting in his kitchen eating a ham sandwich with spicy brown mustard and he's tossing bits of cold chicken to his gang of cats thinking about the bills he has to pay, Mary's thighs, a new piston for his boat, things past being present, his upset stomach, the last thing Castro told him and how when Castro told the truth his cigar sang and when he told a lie it was silent and Castro spoke saying there was this Jew, a physicist. He survived the revolution. He survived the civil war. He survived the war when it started again. Khrushchev said he was the greatest genius nut he ever met. There were rumors that Trotsky had hired a double. An imposter was in Mexico, having it on with Frieda and so on, and it was driving Stalin crazy. He just couldn't stand the tension. At the same time this report catches his eye. It's about the second St. Petersburg, that is the other Petrograd or Leningrad or whatever. You see Stalin had ordered the construction of a second city, a second Saint Petersburg, a duplicate, an urban echo to be built in the middle of nowhere in Siberia or somewhere under a mountain, and in it they locked up all the geniuses and they locked up all the actors to play the roles of people in the city just as if it were the real place. The geniuses included mathematicians and physicists, artists and actors and engineers because Stalin said we must find a way to institutionalize creativity, and one of them was this fellow, this physicist Lazar, and Lazar had studied ancient books. He had a collection of texts going back to the Middle Ages, books that were copies of even older books and in one of them he found a treatise for a machine, an incredible machine that it was said, had first been built by Archimedes and had been known by Solomon himself and this machine had only been built once and then lost and all that remained were the diagrams which were incomplete and Lazar, Katzenberg, that was his name; Lazar Katzenberg, he called it the Super Atomic Piston Ring, and he said, it was a machine that would allow the user to tap into conversations anywhere in the world at any moment in time. But there was a problem: it selected the time and the place and the conversation at random and it had the habit of jumping to another conversation without warning. But, Stalin was so anxious to find the real Trotsky that he ordered all available resources to be devoted to the project and he ordered all the military men who knew about it to be killed which is the real reason for the purges of the thirties, and so Lazar went to work, and they built the damn thing and it started to work and you can imagine who was more relieved, Lazar or Stalin, but history as we know has its own tricks as comrade Twain said and the machine began to do unexpected things. It began to jump and this they expected, but it also began recording itself while jumping. You see, it existed within and on a time line just like the other time lines and from moment to moment it would jump and so it was sometimes as if they were staring into a hall of mirrors watching themselves watch themselves and Lazar wrote a journal, Khrushchev said, of which they never found more than one volume though they knew there had to be others and Lazar, he said it was a wilderness of mirrors—that was what he called it—and he said it was like the old adage about a thousand monkeys typing on a thousand typewriters and how eventually they would reproduce the complete works of Shakespeare because they began to see that they could build files, enormous files that held everything ever said from one person to another. But the files were always disjointed and constructed subjectively with lines from one conversation crossing over another so that it was as if there was really just one conversation that had neither beginning nor end and they spent hour upon hour, year after year, trying to understand what was being said and they built a great warehouse to hold the stories and then another and then another until they ran out of room though there was still always something else to listen to, so they began to dig a tunnel under a mountain—a tunnel that went on forever and still there was more to record and there was an elaborate process for moving the files which required a Byzantine system of clearances and registered secrets and secrets built up inside other secrets until they came around in a circle and met each other which required a whole new set of secrets until you had a system that was infinite but complete, and the place they were stored became its own city with the army of clerks and guards called Xanadu until catastrophe hit them—it began to record Stalin himself and they had to tell him and Stalin was faced with a terrible dilemma. There he was sitting on the greatest instrument in history and it was working on him as well as everyone else. But he couldn't shut it down he was addicted to the information, to hearing the wheels of creation turning with such precision and the whole time he had one great obsession: Trotsky—where Trotsky was, where in the whole world the real Trotsky was and at the same time he couldn't afford to let anyone know that Trotsky was in hiding somewhere and not in Mexico. But he couldn't shut the machine down nor leave it running and in the end it killed him—the stress of it and you know, one night at Khrushchev's dacha, we were sitting by the fire and Khrushchev had told the whole crazy story and he said it was the eye of god. You can imagine it there at the center of world revolution: me and Khrushchev discussing the eye of god like a couple of wobbly-kneed Jesuit school boys, but that's what he said—the eye of god' and Castro stopped there with a great dramatic flourish puffing once precisely on his cigar. It was late then and dark on the balcony of the presidential palace with only the faint red tip of the cigar and the light from within Castro's study forming an irregular square on the cool white tiles of the floor and the guards were shadows within shadows within the within of the night hanging as a glove over the earth and Hemingway sat staring at the sixth toe on the right front paw of his twelfth cat and smelled the scent of Castro's cigar, the scent of the heat, lazy, warm and sensual as anything true and knowable and he thought: what a story, what a story and then, stroking his cat on the chin, he thought about Castro's eyes, walked to his study, and began to write.

ॐॐ

Tiresias Considers

"Justice is incidental to law and order."

— J. Edgar Hoover

ℰℛ

The Package Arrives

Once upon a time in the time of the country of the novel Raymond parked his car at the top of the drive. There were three other cars parked there and a man in a chauffeur's uniform was cleaning them. He stopped and looked at Ray as he got out of his car. Ray stared at him and the man stared back and then the chauffer looked away and Ray thought he looked like a man who had been caught playing with a doll.

ℰℛ

The General was in his study. He was examining his map of heaven. He had a protractor and a compass and a mechanical pencil. In a ledger, he listed many names. His butler came into the study and said that Mr. Chandler had arrived.

ℰℛ

—The problem, said the General, is that a name has fallen off the list of conversations. I need to find it. Everything is being recorded. But if you listen to everything you hear nothing. Still, it is a most delicate and dangerous situation. We must return the name to the list.

—You should be more careful, said Ray.

—Yes, said the General, but these things happen.

Ray looked at the General and his big fluffy ears. He thought the General would not be so careless and he wondered who had taken the name from the list. The General sipped his tea. It was warm in the study.

—Are you the only one with access to the list?

—Yes, said the General.

—No one from the studio? Staff?

—No one, said the General.

The door to the study opened and the butler came in and walked quietly to the General's side, bent at the waist and whispered in the General's fluffy ear. The General wrinkled his nose and the butler turned, walked out and closed the door.

✍ ☙

—You live alone?

—No, my daughters sometimes, said the General. My wife died a few years ago. The rain.

—I'll speak to them, said Ray.

—My attorney, Mr. Herman, will answer your questions.

Ray looked at the General. The General looked at Ray and then he looked his watch. They discussed money. Then the General stopped Ray as he was leaving.

—The list, he said, is very old. From time to time names fall from the list and we endeavor to find them. The issue here is that, as I am retired, losing a name from the list is somewhat more problematic than it might have been previously.

Ray stood in the doorway regarding the General.

—It would be viewed as my fault, said the General. My daughters would be put at a distinct disadvantage were it made public that a name had fallen from the list. It would cause some embarrassment for some of my former associates.

—This would be a lot easier if you told me what you're not telling me and just said it directly.

—There is a lawyer, said the General.

—Isn't there always a lawyer? said Ray.

—His name is Guzman, said the General as if Ray had not spoken. Were he to find the name it would make things complicated. It would be as if we had all fallen through the looking glass.

—Well, said Ray, I'll be in touch. Whether or not I find a lost little girl or a Jabberwalk.

The General gave a slight smile and his ears twitched.

☙❧

Outside at the top of the winding drive the chauffeur was cleaning the cars and he still looked like a man who had been caught playing with dolls. Ray ignored him and got in his car. He took his tobacco pouch from the glove compartment and his pipe from his jacket pocket, tapped a pinch into the bowl, put the pouch away and struck the two matches he took from a small box he kept in his trousers at once, regarded the rising blue-yellow flare of the lit sulfur and drew the flame down into the pipe, stepped on the gas and drove out on to the street as the tall gate of the General's estate closed behind him.

☙❧

Like Shit on a Stick

I'm in a bar on Thomas Street. Ariel walks in and sits down on a stool next to me. I stare at him staring at me in the mirror at the back of the bar. He orders a beer.

—Well, he says, Europe was fantastic.

I stare at my drink.

—I'm giving a lecture about it at Duke. You should come.

I stare at the grooves in the bar-top.

—You know your idea about why Robert Cohen wears spectacles?

I look at him in the mirror. He's smiling and staring back at me and he waits while the bartender brings him his beer.

—I'm delivering a paper on it. It's called Spectacles and testicles: Hemingway's humor and the hidden truth.

I stared at my hands. They seemed to belong to someone else. He drank his beer.

—Next month I'm going to see this girl I met. One of the twins. I read her your story. You know the one they used in that show about the people who work at the White House. And also the one about the word scutt they used in that show about the doctors. She thinks I'm brilliant. She likes to give me blow-jobs while I read to her.

He laughed and drank his beer.

—I've been reading your posts by the way. In the end, you must realize it's hopeless. If you ever do get recognition they'll destroy you. They'll blackmail someone into saying you fuck little boys or sheep or both. They'll get someone to say you turned Audrey out to pay for your coke or your weed. They'll accuse you of plagiarism which of course will be the supreme irony. You can post and pretend you're someone else on as many discussion pages as you like. You can pretend to be Bonaparte at Austerlitz or Faulkner on the Jordan. It's hopeless. You've become like Billy Pilgrim jumping through time and memory. It's hopeless. Give up.

I stared at my hands. I imagined that they had detached from my wrists but there was no blood, no pain. They flapped out into the bar and out the door and down the street and went over the Golden Gate and in the fog they vanished and it was very quiet.

—You know you look like shit on a stick. When was the last time you slept?

He finished his beer and tossed a twenty on the bar. He stood and looked at himself in the mirror.

—Give it up. It's like you're waiting for a message from the emperor. It's never going to come and you'll just spend your life sitting by the window waiting.

He smiled again; looked in the mirror and walked out to the street.

ʊ ʊ

Castro's Pants

Clyde Tolson's nickname for J. Edgar Hoover was Speedy. The spasm of violence that propelled Hoover to fear everything and everyone lurched like an angry hermaphrodite with delicate hands, and the files grew and grew and the president came to Hoover's house which had been Hoover's mother's house and they stood in the basement, which had been turned into a kind of adolescent den, and Hoover showed the president files that contained examples of what Hoover called filth, because filth was the engine of his soul in that he felt dirty, truly unclean and he showed him the pictures and the president mumbled and snorted appropriate words of outrage, and they drank glasses of milk and ate ham sandwiches on white bread (and the president was afraid) and Fidel Castro becomes a great cigar wrapped within the leaves of all things Cuba, and he recounts the story of running in the snow with Nikita Khrushchev and how laughing, Khrushchev had tried to stuff snow down Castro's pants because they had to decide who was on top and who was on the bottom because history is a question of where you draw the boundary or border of narrative, and who defines the boundary or the border is the one telling the story.

ॐ ॐ

Speed Freaks

—What we want, said Turpentine, is for you to keep an eye on him; get close to his girlfriend.

—Utta? She's a drunk. A speed freak.

—Then, said Turpentine, drink with her. Only, get close to him. Let me know who he knows.

—He's queer, you know that, don't you? Sometimes he has the girl. Sometimes he gets crippling cramps in his feet and he can't move for hours. I think it's psychosomatic.

—Sure, we know all about that.

They were sitting in a bar drinking beers. Turpentine was wearing a baseball cap and sunglasses and the other man who was named Herman was wearing a rumpled white linen suit. It was warm and the street was lit with festive lights strung from the lamp posts and over the fronts of the bars that lined the street.

—He's writing a novel, said Herman, I don't know what it's about.

—I'd like to see a copy, said Turpentine.

—I can't copy it.

—I'll get you a camera, a very small camera. And something else.

Herman looked at Turpentine.

—I'll get you some Benzedrine. She does Benzedrine, right?

—Yea, said Herman, all day. But lately, it's been tequila.

—Tequila is easy. I'll get the stuff, you give it to her.

—They'll want to know who I'm buying from.

—Well, said Turpentine, that's perfect. When they ask you, let me know. I'll take care of it.

Herman looked down the street and saw people coming and going and someone waving a white sparkler in the air, the sparks shooting off in silver streaks and then brightly white popping in the dark.

✷ ✷

The Beautiful Fall Colors

She was writing a letter and saying how beautiful the fall colors were and that she was bored and Herman was looking at the books in the bookshelf and he was waiting for her to say she was done and he was thinking about New York—he missed it and he did not like Mexico and he did not like Mexico City—and then she was done and standing in the doorway between the sitting room and the bedroom where she had been writing the letter.

—I have something for you, Utta, said Herman.

She was standing against the door frame holding a glass in her hands. She was tired and she smiled tentatively and she saw the inhalers in his hand and he was smiling.

✷ ✷

Winter, West Berlin, 1989

In a forest in a clearing there is a statue, an enormous statue of a man and I ask her what it is but she rushes away from it down the path saying, whispering, 'It's nothing. The war, the first war...' and then we walked down to the river. The water was still, the air was so tight with the cold it was as if we were walking through something enveloping us, pressing in on us, making everything slow, heavy. The water was grey and then blue. Our breath came in great white plumes that faded into the grey air and across from the trees. Across the river, there was a large house and from the pole on the roof, a large union jack snapped back and forth in the wind.

The Wall

That winter the wall came down and Germany laughed and Grass cried and we walked in the forest looking over a river coldly gray flecked with white as if bones of memory were drifting by... That winter she was wearing a long black coat, her collar up and her black scarf, the air tightly thick, slowly thickening with the winter and across the river was a great house flying the Union Jack hanging down limply in the still air. I kissed her, her tongue warmly moist, wrapping around mine and lips cold, warming together wetly thickening and blooming our skin cold to the touch. We were very happy. The trees were bare, their branch spines making fractured patterns in the air and the sky, a still blue slate without clouds.

We walked in the woods along the river until we came to the road and she said we should go across the road and we did. On the other side was a gate and down from the gate, a narrow road and at the bottom of the road was a small square.

On one side was a low building like a long barn and in it there was a wedding party and people coming and going, laughter thrilling inside the still cold air with music. Across the square was another building—low like a great farm house and inside was a bar. We went in and through the front door between a great gray wool blanket hanging between the outer doors and the doors opening to the bar and across the bar we could see a long window with rows of tables and chairs and through the windows you could see the river and a dock for boats.

We sat beside the windows. Outside was a man at the side of a sail boat. I watched him working a long rope, splicing it with a thick blade and his breath coming and going into the still air in a thick cloud of thickly undulating white plumes that faded in the cold above the slow moving river, itself drifting so very slow, deeply gray cold while a fallen branch from a tree drifted down on the slow current, only two-thirds of it showing above the surface as an idea for every hidden pulse of the earth.

We ordered drinks and the waiter was crisply happy to get them. He wore a clean white apron and the bar was still, empty except for us. Outside the winter sky was precisely blue.

☙❧

She said there are three possibilities and each is an alternative narrative about the same story. She looked out the window. She looked back and said this is how it is every time we meet.

—How many times have we met?

—Oh, she said, it is impossible to tell anymore. Everything repeats including everyone forgetting and then remembering they have forgotten. The earth is senile. You want to get off the wheel but you can't.

—And what happens?

—In the first story, you stay here with me and you will be a spy in the story of your own life and it will be a German film with subtitles in other languages and there will be many obscure references to alternate realities which shall echo this one as if all the narratives were crossing over and through each other. The narrative will be sequential but non-linear. Someone will think you are a spy. Then they will offer you a job. When you refuse they will threaten you. You will try to leave. Etcetera. Sameness without change.

—And the second?

—And in the second one, you will stay with your glorious Bathsheba in Jerusalem and you will remember me and be a spy in the story of your own life. And there will be many obscure references to alternate narratives, *et cetera*....

—The third?

—And in the third one, you will live elsewhere with a woman who asks about me and takes my name when you make love and there you will be a spy in the story of your own life and you will remember us and in each story you will be a victim of circumstances beyond your control.

Her voice came in a long whisper and her breath snapped under her scarf and she said,

—Now I am the crone, and I have told you your fortune like Madam Sosostris and you will choose and the story will resolve itself into its appropriate form and it will have one accent or another and I will tell you how it is with me and when you tell people the story they will say, 'but no, it is not possible to be a character in a foreign film!' because they are all fictions.

—And how will I answer them?

—You will tell them the story and it will be like the oldest stories with stories within, each one inside the next because we repeat ourselves and instead of chapters in a pretty row there will be the chaos of memory intruding into the present. There will be no plot which is itself a kind of plot and people will say, but where is the plot, and you will smile enigmatically.

—Is that fate?

—Fate is other people.

ॐॐ

German Expressionism

When she was younger she sang and her lover was a man who arranged for her to sing in clubs. That was in Berlin, when the city was still divided.

She has a cassette. It is a recording of her singing in a club. Later she had throat cancer and she stopped singing. She almost never listens to the cassette and she never allows anyone else to hear it. This is called sadness. It has many forms.

She remembered later how the American came to the city and said he was a Berliner too and everyone cheered. She said: I read a story. In the story President DeGaulle returns to Paris and stands upon a balcony of the palace and the people cheer. His assistant says it is wonderful. DeGaulle waves and smiles and he says to the assistant, 'Yes, look at the crowd. I recognize those faces... there... fascist, collaborator, informant, collaborator, fascist. Listen to them cheer.'

When she was young her lover took her home to his small apartment. She had sung at a club. She wore a crisp white man's dress shirt and black stretch pants and ballet flats. She smoked American cigarettes. They made love. They fucked. She observed the differences and the similarities between the two. They listened to American jazz. She discovered Coltrane. She discovered she was pregnant. She discovered her lover was an informant for the police. That was when she was divided against herself and became two people who were one. Later when she learned to laugh a little about it she would say she had a child with Coltrane.

One day, on the island, on the beach, below a long line of trees, she says that her daughter is only a few years younger than I am. 'It is,' she says, whispering, 'so very silly. Why' she says, 'are you so young and I am so old?' I do not answer her. I have no answer. The sea is blue. The sky is the sky.

A man comes along the beach on a donkey. The man is an albino. He wears a big hat with a wide brim. He is selling watermelons. A line of sea birds glide past us parallel to the shore. She says, 'It is like being trapped in a Duras novel and knowing it.'

༄༅

The Hall of Mirrors Part II

(Field Notes Upon the Effects of Quantum Coffee)

Adler is waiting outside the café and he sees Freud appear on the corner across the street. A tram comes by and when it passes, he sees Freud come across the street to meet him.

—Good to see you, says Adler, with a polite bow.

—Likewise, says Freud, also bowing.

Inside the café they order coffee and they discuss different things until Adler again brings up the story about the man claiming truthfully to be an impostor.

—Yes, says Freud, an hysteric.

Adler sips his coffee. He has been having a series of dreams and he is debating sharing them. He looks across the café. There is a man sitting at a table writing in a notebook. Across from him on the table-top there is a saucer and a cup of what Adler assumes is hot coffee. Steam rises from the cup and he watches the thin drape of white-gray vapor float into the atmosphere. They are alone in the café. He turns to his companion.

—Do you know who that is?

—Hmm yes. Ferenczi actually knows him. A novelist. German fellow.

—Oh no, says Adler, not at all. I know who you mean. That's all wrong. Look at this fellow. He's far too young. That's the mathematician. Gödel is his name. Johannes Gödel. A graduate student I knows says he knows him, says he's a genius.

—No, that is the man Ferenczi pointed out to me.

—Well, certainly he may have done so but that does not prove his identity. Besides my chess partner knows him.

—The hysteric?

—Yes, but–

—Ferenczi was quite confident. He was on his way to speak with the mother of one of his patients and we quite literally bumped into that man.

—Well, no matter then.

—Yes.

—You know the thing is I've been considering the idea that there's a sort of Zeno's paradox to everything we've been discussing and my relationship with the actor.

—Yes?

—If memory is a constant, absorbing what it experiences or an infinite library constantly rearranging things on the shelves, then time is a paradox and now is also before and before is also now. Thus memory is also a paradox.

—We have not discussed this issue. As you know memory exists in a non-time sphere that we call the past.

—Yes, as I was saying I've been–

—We have certain ideas.

—Yes, as if this were an axiom. I mean about the nature of memory—narrative strategies are called into question. I mean all sets that define consciousness and or identity are neither here nor not here, neither completely true nor absolutely false. The mind is an arrow that never reaches its target as every act of understanding instantly flies apart into arrow and target, present and past both at once and listening to people tell you about themselves means you are instantly incorporated into a four-dimensional space-time consisting of your now and before and their now and before, which has us conclude that–

But there he had to stop as all of a sudden Freud lurched forward and said in a seething whisper, my god-damned foot, and slid down in his chair as Adler lurched forward in alarm to ask what was wrong.

—A cramp, he said through his clenched teeth.

—A cramp?

—Yes, I must walk it off.

He stood stiffly measuring how much weight to place on his foot and then he marched to the door and went outside while Adler gathered his coat and went to follow him. On his way out, he looked back and saw that the man he was sure was Gödel was gone and the girl who worked there was clearing up the table placing two cups and two saucers on a tray.

Special Effects

—What we want, said Herman, speaking as if from a script, is a television show—a whole group of shows that make our agents sound cool, ruthlessly hip to what's now to pop slang and culture, aware of other television shows, past and present, and cool references to music and movies. Obscure, but not too obscure. It's patriotic. And a story about racism. A heroic preacher or something... in Georgia... and it's got integrity, the whole show has integrity. And a show about lesbians, really hot lesbians who are also spies working for us to track down the bad guys. And they make cool jokes about hip films and one of them mentions designer brands and they have a lot of books in their house and one of them is reading The Garden of Eden and you see the titles of the book on the shelves. We'll provide a list and one of the girls has to have eidetic memory. And the other likes modern poetry or jazz. You know, so they seem genuine. That's a key plot line.

—We can do that. We can make them say anything you want. We have–

—We have our own ideas for dialogue.

—Sure, said Mr. Bob, how do you–

—We will provide advisors, said Herman.

—Advisors, said Mr. Bob.

—Yes, said Herman.

—Patriotic, said Mr. Bob.

—For the war, said Herman.

—Support the troops, said Mr. Bob, the studio wants to cooperate.

✍ ✌

Tiresias Defiant

"The cure for crime is not the electric chair, but the high chair."

— J. Edgar Hoover

✍ ✌

Audrey Resplendent

Audrey, a brutalized whore one moment, a goddess the next. Do we ever escape from clichés? Do we ever escape from ourselves?

On a Greek island with Audrey, climbing up the side of the highest mountain: A large rock slips loose from under my boot and with a terrific echoing crack, as if of a bat and a ball. It flies through the air and as I am saying, look out, it arcs just to the side of her head, just to the side of becoming Joan Vollmer.

☙❧

Who Done it?

Ariel was writing a screenplay based upon the novel. In it were all the characters that would become famous. He wrote about the twins and he wrote about the spies, the gangsters and the lawyer. He wrote about the artist and he wrote about himself and when he came to the story about the dead chauffer he realized he did not know why the man was dead or who had killed him.

He spoke to the director. The director did not know either. He spoke to the star and the star did not know. He called the author who said, I don't know but I'll think about it and get back to you.

But there was no time to wait and Ariel was on a deadline so he wrote the story the best way he knew how and when he was done he stood by the window listening to music and watched the rain come down streaking the windows in long lines of red.

☙❧

It is all Original

The Man from Hope goes on a talk show. Everything is perfectly scripted and tightly choreographed. Then all at once, seemingly from nowhere, he sputters, his face growing red and puffy, fleshy and large, he says (about his book) this is all original material, and the host, with concern borne of confusion says, 'Of course it is,' his voice calm, reassuring, as if to say, why, why in the world would you think that anyone would ever think otherwise? Why are so many people from the top of the political food chain answering questions no one is asking?

☒ ☒

Tiresias Confirms

"We are a fact-gathering organization only. We don't clear anybody. We don't condemn anybody."
— J. Edgar Hoover

☒ ☒

What the Water Said

The hood and the loss of light. Tied down to a board lifted up and back she is coughing water, spitting mangled words. With her heart racing and her hands shaking, she pisses over her thighs and her skin feels heat and her head is shaking so hard it smacks the board in an awkward staccato rhythm while a voice softly says 'Just tell us what we want to know,' and she spits, snot flying from her nose into her mouth, she coughs phlegm, tears, and the sweat pours over her head and covers her face. She hears people laughing making a wager about time and duration she shits herself and vomits and then swallows her bile, coughing, choking... She is drowning and the soft voice says, 'Just tell us what we want to know, what we already know. Do you know what we know? Tell us.' She coughs, bites her tongue, tastes blood and water, bile, stinging stomach acid. She pukes on herself and then the voice says again '...what we know, tell us' and she is weeping, hysterically coughing, shaking, vomiting and the water says, 'Tell us what we want to know, just tell us what we want to know.'

☒☒

Each of the major uses of violence produced characteristic forms of organization. War making yielded armies, navies, and supporting services. State making produced durable instruments of surveillance and control within the territory.

— Charles Tilly

The Last Drive

—Look Ray, said Lt. Mulreavy, no one cares who killed the damn chauffeur.

—So you're just here for the view? Or because you still believe in the plot?

Mulreavy laughed, but the laughter did not reach his gray eyes. He sat across from Ray and looked at the chess board on the table.

—You have the name or you don't, said Mulreavy.

—Name? I got a phonebook full of names. You need one?

—Ray, you want to be thinking hard about this. Being a character is no way to be.

—Thinking is overrated. And character is everything.

Mulreavy put a big hand on the black king. He stared at it like a hungry man contemplating a steak.

—I got people at the studio, said Mulreavy. They are making trouble Ray. You might want to reconsider your attitude. There's a war you know.

—There's always a war, said Ray; it's like saying there's weather.

—You being smart with me?

—Oh lieutenant, you know I could never be smart with you. I'm just saying we're into reruns, same story over and over again fresh from the studio and everyone acts like it's brand new.

Mulreavy stood up and it was like watching a elephant stand up and it just kept standing up and then it stood up some more after that and he looked down at Ray and the black king seemed to get very small in the lieutenant's big hand.

—I can only protect you Ray if you help me. Keep being smart and we might just hang the chauffeur's death on someone.

—You want to put the king back where he belongs, said Ray.

—Sure Ray, sure. He goes on the square where he belongs with all the other pieces.

—Come and visit me again sometime lieutenant; it's been a treat.

Mulreavy put the king down on the board. He turned and walked to the door. He stopped and looked back at Ray.

—Guzman's not your friend Ray. You keep this up you won't have any friends at all.

—In proportion as he simplifies his life, the laws of the universe will appear less complex, and solitude will not be solitude, nor poverty, nor weakness.

—That supposed to mean something to me?

—Just a slogan from Mr. Walden.

—You want to guard against being too clever Ray. No one likes a smartass.

Ray picked up the black king.

—The king's got no conscience to be caught

lieutenant. You might want to remember that.

Mulreavy adjusted his hat, opened the door and closed it behind him as he stared down the steps to the street and Ray put the king back on the board and thought about a drink.

☙☞

Contents Under Pressure

A man came running down the street. He was vomiting the truth. Everyone scattered; everyone ran.

It was raining and the rain was red. The man was running. Perhaps he was running from someone.

Eventually, he passed out on the sidewalk. Then they took him away in an ambulance. The lights flashed red and blue and the red rain was streaked with long lines of blue from the flashing lights.

They turned a hose on the street and the sidewalk where the man had spewed great puddles of the truth. The water from the hose ran white then red and the streets were red and the puddles were a suet of all the colors. A few people stared. Soon, the puddles were gone. It was as if they had never existed.

☙☞

Utta & Mattya

Their mother went to Rome. This was before she was their mother but still, she was their mother. This is mysterious but true. She met a man in Rome. He was a doctor. He was from her home town. They agreed it was mysterious that they should come from the same place and not know each other and then both arrive in Rome and meet at a church open to tourists.

Later, after she was pregnant, he said goodbye. She wanted him to say goodbye. She was ashamed to have become pregnant. She was pleased to be ashamed. This central paradox of her existence informed the arc of her life from beginning to end with frequent stops in-between in places marked broadly upon the map of her soul.

This was always hard for most people to understand. The man she married, and who adopted the girls never understood, but he was blessed with a low intelligence and a high opinion of his generosity, and as he had power and was ruthless, it did not bother him.

However, for the girls, it was a magnificent disaster.

☞☜

In the beginning it was clear that the girls, who were identical twins, were going to be great beauties, but of a mysterious sort. To look at them was to be perplexed. The nose was too long and the chin too wide and there was a mole small and black like a strange button or exotic spandrel that sat at the corner of the right side of the chin like some idea that had been left over from the moment of creation and for which no one could find a use.

And then there were the eyes. The long thick arching eyebrows and the long elongated serpentine eyes that said yes and no and perhaps and everything in-between and often with a strange self-awareness and intelligence and a vast open space into which people were pulled and from which came a cold, earnest fury for which there was no solution and from which only one person ever escaped.

The bodies were long and firm and lean and the hair, a magnificent waterfall of richly dark strands of secret ideas and whispers and sex and the scent of something impossible.

They should not have been beautiful, but they were; and they did not know it truthfully for a long time so that they suffered at the hands of other children who did not understand their mysterious ways or how they seemed to know things just by seeing a gesture or a pair of shoes. They learned eventually and men started to fall at their feet like wounded ideas that slowly bled to death and were briefly resurrected by a word or a touch and the two of them soon discovered that they loved sex, that they needed it, that they relished it, and so they embraced it and nothing, not food or clothes or ideas, ever made them as happy as when they could come again and again and again upon having the realization that sex was due to arrive; the anticipation of touch and embrace and the moment when there was someone at the door or waiting expectantly somewhere, anywhere; waiting for them to arrive.

And of course, for a long time, they were tormented by this because they were their mother's creation and she hated them and loved having them to hate and when she looked at them she saw Rome and she hated Rome and she hated the man who had got her pregnant except that she loved him more than anyone or anything because he had given her the thing she hated most in all the world which was her identity and the labyrinth that was her identity curled around and around and twisted into a conundrum of such magnitude and such complexity that the only way it could be contained was for her to hide it away in a purse which itself had so many secret chambers and mysterious compartments that in the end the girls knew it was a portal to some other dimension and when they were old enough, she began to buy them purses and often would buy many at once and keep one for herself and give the others to her daughters who kept them in their boxes in their closets wrapped in fine colored tissue and all the purses hummed and buzzed and each was an epic poem without beginning or end.

ᢒᢙ

Mattya at the Hospital

Ariel was addicted to heroin. He checked himself into a clinic to kick it. The clinic was known to offer a cure to addicts. The clinic was funded by the Ministry. Ariel did not know that. No one, except the men from the Ministry knew that, and it was to be decades before anyone found out the truth.

But that is a story for another time and place where things make sense. For example: Ariel was in the hospital. He shared a room with a man who had been taken to the hospital for vomiting the truth. One day they were talking in the garden of the hospital across from the petting zoo. The zoo was the idea of a man who had been the hospital's first patient. He came from a wealthy family. He said, 'I come from money,' as if money were a place or a thing that gave birth to other things.

Of course, that is true about money.

So, he donated a menagerie of animals for a petting zoo because he thought it would help people and sometimes it did.

So, Ariel and the man who vomited the truth were sitting on a bench watching a goat with big curving horns rub his horns against a tree trunk and then, on the other side of the low metal fence that ran around the petting zoo inside the walled courtyard of the hospital, they both saw a tall thin woman, in a beautiful red coat walk by and stop and stare at the goat and they both fell at her feet like wounded ideas and she saw them and she knew in that instant that she could have either of them or neither or both together at once or separately rotating them as if on a merry-go-round and the goat had yellow eyes and his horns were golden-brown.

☙ ❧

—It came out all at once, said the man.

Mattya was looking at him intently and she knew he was thinking two things. The first thing he was thinking was that he desperately wanted someone to talk to about how he had vomited the truth. The second thing he was thinking was that he wanted to glide his cock over Mattya's lips and see her swallow his cum but as an abstraction without passion or pain or desire but more like a drawer where the silverware is placed in precise rows. She knew these two things were exchanging places in his mind and above them, high above the city, damp clouds drifted by in the shape of a car and a giraffe and an ornate box with a round cover.

—I was at home making a pot of coffee, he said, and then all at once it came out of me in a great gush and I thought I was going to die. It splashed against the counter and the floor of the kitchen and then I ran from the house and went down the street puking the truth.

—It must have been terrifying, said Mattya.

The man looked up at the clouds. He thought about how Mattya's face must look when she had an orgasm.

—It had complete control over me, he said. I was powerless.

He looked at her; she looked at him.

—Why are you here? he asked.

She looked away and stared at the ground.

—I want to be useful, she said.

—Useful? Everyone is useful in the end.

—I feel useless.

—I am taking these pills. The doctors give them to me every morning. I haven't thrown up in two weeks.

—Do you feel better?

—I don't feel anything.

—What is it like?

He stared at the ground. He stared at the wall of the courtyard. He stared at her elegant blue boots.

—It's like being inside of yourself and you know you're inside yourself, but every time you try to be yourself a space opens between you and your own mind. And then there are your thoughts and they just come with the regularity of a bus or a train. But there is nothing good and nothing bad. The train comes, the train goes.

—I'm jealous, she said.

—I don't know what that means, he said, and he smiled. But the smile was not attached to the rest of his face and it seemed to move a little as if she were watching someone try on a suit that didn't fit. Then the smile went away and all the remained was the face, bloodless and still.

✍ ✋

I Pendulum

I watch the new television shows. I watch the one about the twins and the writer. It gets excellent reviews. I drift from despair to melancholy. Sometimes I laugh. Sometimes when I think about the time that has been stolen from me, I drag a knife over my wrists to see how much pain I can endure. Wherever I have lived, I examine the roof to see if it is high enough so that if I jump I can be certain that I will not survive the fall.

I no longer know what normal is or how it feels. I am a story that never stops telling itself. I am a story that has no end other than giving up or starting over again.

Someone asks me what I want and I can only say, I want to go away.

✍ ❧

Ariel and Mattya

—I'm writing a novel, said Ariel.

—About what?

He looked at Mattya and smiled. They were both smoking cigarettes and they were sitting on a bench just outside of the hospital. Ariel was allowed out for an hour and within a week he was to be considered for discharge. A car went by and sliced through a puddle of red rain water.

—It's a place. It's in a place that has no name and these women go to the river to wash their clothes and a body washes up and it's the body of a man, a woman's husband who had disappeared years before. And soon, one after another of the missing washes up and the women demand to bury them and the army won't let them. There is a writer—a reporter—he's there working on one story when he walks into this other story. But the police, the secret police, blackmail him and force him to write a different version of the story. However, every morning, just before he's to show them the alternate version, he rereads what he's written and discovers it's changed and reverted to the original. Of course it all becomes very complicated. The secret police are recording everything. They find a man, a writer, and they begin to record him and they discover that he knows he is being recorded so he speaks into the microphone, but the things he says and the stories he tells are things that the spies know are secrets and they begin to follow him everywhere and he sees them and they can't understand how he can see them nor can they understand how he knows their secrets and they listen to everything he says and they decide that he is giving them a secret code and they make stories out of it and they put it on television as if it were a beacon to attract people who knew the code and they make sure the shows receive excellent reviews and the shows that work are copied and the copies are copied and so on as if it were all a vast hall of mirrors replicating itself and in it they listen to everything, but hear nothing.

He stopped. He smoked. He looked at Mattya.

—May I read it?

—Yes, he said, of course.

They sat quietly for a while, smoking. Another car went by and the red rain water splashed up and onto the sidewalk.

—I am fascinated by something I read, said Ariel. I'm going to work it into the novel.

Mattya loved books. She wanted to write a novel herself. She wanted to write a book like *Death in the Cathedral* or the *Savage Detectives*. She loved the idea that Ariel was a writer. She loved that he was addicted to heroin and that he was in a hospital because of it and it all felt genuine and full of mystery and something that might be dangerous and true because it was dangerous and the more she felt afraid, the truer everything felt and so she felt the strange soft terror of those things that in contrast had become false all the more intensely.

She dropped her cigarette on the ground next to the other one she smoked, stepping on it and then took another from the box she had and lit it and looked very dramatic and beautiful with her long black hair falling down over the bright red scarf she was wearing.

She looked at Ariel and asked him to tell her what was so fascinating. He made her wait.

—I read about this man, he said, and there was this sort of biography of him. He was a writer. The line was, 'then he had his leg amputated, and his health improved.' It is so brutal and fascinating.

Her eyes were wide and her face was full of something deep and mysterious that might have been joy or passion or fear or all of those things at once or perhaps was something else that had no name or did, but was unknown to anyone in this story, so she stared and he stared and in that moment, he knew he would have her and he smiled and she smiled and she knew in that moment she would have him and together they thought about the man who had his leg amputated and whose health improved because of it.

So every week she came and they spoke and he told her the story about the man who lost his leg.

—And then while he was recuperating at a hospital, he met another patient who had wandered over from the sanitarium where he was being treated he said for a complaint of the lungs. He was a mysterious man with old world manners and conceits and who one day said, 'Will you pretend to know me? I am being followed,' he said, 'by the Czar's police. I am a physicist and I have escaped from the Second Petersburg. If you help me I will tell you an incredible story and show you the most amazing device ever invented.'

Well, of course the man was torn. On the one hand, though his health was better, he was also miserable about his leg and instantly hated the old-man with his crazy story and he thought how ugly and repugnant the man was with his old man hands clutching his plain black box which he said was a wondrous invention, and he hated his old-man saggy skin and his wattle neck and would have sent him away but instead, and for no reason he could explain, agreed to pretend he knew the old man.

They made plans to meet near the fountain in the interior courtyard tomorrow. And the next day, they were going to meet and he was on his way eagerly you could say, when another patient stopped him. He leaned in over the man's wheelchair and said:

—That old man is crazy. I wouldn't speak to him if I were you. A man in your condition must be mindful. One false move and the wrong people know you exist. Right after that it's whoops and your taking a dive off a balcony.

The man shuffled off without another word and he was stunned. He sat there and then as it had been before, he was persuaded in his own mind that the strangeness of it was too intriguing and these two nuts were having a jug of fun with him and he rolled on to the fountain and there as planned was the old man.

—People, he said, call me Shapinsky, but my real name is Katzenberg.

—Whatever you like.

—You don't believe me?

—I asked the nurse, she said your name is Shapinsky.

—I told them that. I'm telling you something else.

—You admit you're a liar.

—Yes, said the old man, unlike the rest of you hypocrites.

They stared at each other and the man in the chair realized he liked the old nut and he nodded at him.

—Ok, so you have a fancy mysterious box. And a story.

—Oh yes, he said. Yes, I do, and it owns me.

—How's that?

—This, he said, is my puzzle palace.

—A puzzle palace?

—Yes, I am a king who is ruled by his kingdom. I hear everything and understand nothing.

—You always talk this way?

The old man smiled. His hands were small and tight on the box.

—If you prefer, we could make claw marks upon the wall.

—What about it then?

—I've been watching you.

—Of course.

—What do you mean by that?

—Do you think I'm some sort of functional illiterate? These stories always have characters like you—crazy old wise-guys who have amazing stories about albatrosses and haunted castles or men who have sold their shadows. It's the same routine every damn time. Elaborate metaphors and symbolic utterances about things no one understands.

—How is that different from anyone else? You could say all that about physicists or politicians?

They stared at each other and then the old man smiled.

—Do you know the *Thousand and One Nights*?

—Of course, said the man with one leg.

—Do you know the story of the three apples?

—Go on.

—The first detective story. Droste really. Written because they had begun to perceive time folding in on itself through perception and repetition and because they had become aware of patterns.

—I thought they were entertainment.

—I did not say they weren't.

—Yes.

—And in one version there is a Vizier to the Caliph. And the Vizier is very powerful. He whispers in the Caliph's ear every day. The Caliph trusts him.

He has three great man-sized boxes in his study each locked and only opened with a special key. In each one, he keeps a copy of the keys and in each, there is something of great value. In the first, he keeps the list of names. He checks it every day to see that new names have been added and to make sure the old ones have not fallen from the list. In the second, he keeps his list of those who eventually he will have silenced. And in the third, he has the blueprints for this.

He stopped and showed the man the box and he pressed a button and the box opened and from a gold spring there came a small figure and it was of a ballerina spinning and in her hand was a small egg and the egg opened and from within the box there came the sound of people speaking and of conversations broken down into waves of sound that flew and circled began ended and began again and sometimes there were names and places and then the man heard a voice he recognized and he focused and listened and soon enough the voice became distinct and he listened to himself asking the old man questions about the box and then he heard the man's voice saying, 'I leave this with you. They will be coming soon to take me to Petersburg to work on a newer version.' And then the box closed and the old man put the box down beside the fountain.

—Goodbye, said the old man.

—No, wait, said the man with one leg, I have a question.

The old man waited.

—Do you, asked the man with one leg, believe we exist in the here and the past?

—A strange question.

—I've been having a recurring dream.

—About the nature of time.

—Yes, in a way. It's always the same; three roads meet and there's been an accident. A death. The police are there but they don't speak. There's a young girl; she just sits there. And there's a sign showing distance and direction. A broken wheel has rolled to the sign from the accident. It looks like the wheel of a carriage.

—In the same instance.

—What?

—The answer to your question. Now and before exist in the same space and every attempt to straighten out the strange loop of it will fail just as if you played Bach with a saw or two hands were trying to trace each other. The answer to the riddle is that it makes no sense.

—What does this mean?

—Everything in the puzzle palace repeats. People repeat themselves. The stories repeat themselves. This is the secret inside the box. This is the secret no one can know. Gilgamesh and the war are forever. You and I have had this conversation before.

—What is the nature of time?

—Time is the crone in the field.

—That's awful.

—Get used to it.

✠☙

Ariel stopped. He closed his notebook. Mattya stared at Ariel and she knew she was in love and love fell over her like a great curtain falling in front of a vast stage.

✠☙

Naked Fedora

> *"The truth may appear, only once..."*
>
> — William Burroughs

✠☙

The Assassin's Hat

We could turn our backs to the threat of reality and listen to music. This is Maryanne in the museum in Berlin. The city is divided. There is an exposition. The surreal holds sway and a large banner snaps in the stiff winter wind. A man in a bowler hat. Consider the danger of the truth.

A man has turned his back upon the men watching him. He has turned away from the threat and he is considering what it means to observe music. The assassins gather and wait and watch and the strong wind of winter blows down the wall and the man in the painting is in another dimension which many people foolishly dismiss as unreal or imagined and she says, whispering, 'It is impossible to distinguish between the danger of reality and dreams.'

☙❧

Walter Benjamin did not know Frieda Kahlo.

Ariel sits on the edge of a bed in an otherwise empty apartment in Tangiers, and stares at his shoe. Perhaps he sits there for an hour or a week. He stares at his shoe (the right shoe not the left, as the left shoe is under the bed) and he hears his typewriter keys being punched, the tell-tale slap of metal on paper and platen.

The story gets up from the table and staggers into the room where Ariel sits on the bed staring at his shoe. The story has long hair and an endless beard and breath that sometimes reeks like an elephant with weeping ulcerous sores.

Ariel's soul reels under the weight of a bout of the delirium tremens, hallucinating people coming out of the telephone. He sees himself standing in front of the telephone. The telephone rings. A hand comes out of the receiver and lifts the phone and hands it to Ariel. He answers it, saying, 'this telephone does not work'.

☡ ☡

He is fucking Utta. He has her bent over a table in the garden of her parent's house near the swimming pool. It is a warm evening towards the end of that summer when the red rain was still in the future of the story and within the story as it was then, Ariel had not yet come to the attention of the rabbit-headed general, but that evening, the evening where he possessed Utta to the depth of her soul, he would find himself feeling as if he were living inside a shoe and within that shoe was a copy of everything that had ever been and having learned that secret he would find himself copied and placed as a copy within the vast library of everything in the world that lived in the mind of the general (with the head of a rabbit) who sat on a chair regarding a long line of fresh cadets and listening to a band play a dramatic marching tune, rhythmically powerful but dead, moving as if it were an animated corpse into which some incredible bellows blew the breath of false life and extraordinarily tortured renditions of reality.

☡ ☡

They Threw the Men from a Great Height into the Sea Below

The church in Rome where they met. She was taking a scarf, a bright red scarf, off her shoulders and was placing it over her head and later, sitting beside a fountain talking, she asked if he liked the scarf and he said yes, that it was always mysterious to him how a scarf is an extension of a woman and how it does nothing to hide anything. He called it paradoxical. They sat there and talked and she handed him the scarf which he touched and smelled and said it had her scent and people came and went in the square by the fountain.

☙ ❧

Utta

Utta said it was as if she were being torn apart from inside.

☙ ❧

Mattya

Mattya said it was as if she were vanishing to a singular point from which every color emerged.

☙ ❧

Surfing in Xanadu

Special Agent Automatic Turpentine went surfing off the coast of Xanadu. Later, while thinking about that one perfect wave, he sat in the bar of the Hotel Majestic sipping ice tea with lemon and across from him was Ariel looking shattered and vacant like an ornate clock that had lost the numbers from its face.

☙ ❧

Herman Dies at the Hotel

—What killed him? asked the first waiter.

—Do not speak about it, said the second waiter.

They were standing on the back patio, looking past the rows of bungalows that faced the sea. Behind them was the hotel. Police dotted the lawn and watched and there were men from the fire brigade pulling on a long thick heavy rope. The rope was tied around a body and the body, bloated, was floating in the surf.

—What difference does it make? the first waiter said. He's still dead.

—His spirit will hear and never leave.

—Superstition, said the second waiter.

—You are too young to be afraid.

—You are too old.

The second waiter crossed himself and said a prayer.

❧❧

Herman at the Hotel & Utta

He stood at the window and conjured Utta in the doorway. She appeared, swaying and reaching for the Benzedrine in his hand. Later he was at the window of his hotel room facing the sea and the sea threw up an endless line of bloated bloody abortions that littered the shore like an army of grotesque and defeated jellyfish.

❧❧

Audrey Smokes

Audrey resplendent in a pair of black kitten-heeled mules and a smile, sits with one elegant leg over the other and smokes a cigarette while I come on her foot.

❧❧

Mattya

I want to feel *all* of your pain.

This is her mantra. She is riding Ariel. She has her

own apartment. Her mother has given her enough money. More than enough. It is a Spartan atmosphere. Everything is neat and neatly arranged and there is nothing ostentatious and there are books—novels and poetry and short story collections and literary magazines and she is riding him ferociously slamming herself into him and she's squealing and whimpering saying 'not yet, not yet, it's too soon' and then she says 'I want to feel all of your pain'.

Later they sit in her kitchen drinking warm strong black tea she has been brewing all day. Perhaps she has succeeding in feeling all of his pain. Perhaps she is made from amber.

In another version of the same story, she tells him about her life and her lovers and how she was married and then only separated from her husband and Ariel refers to him as 'your ex-husband to whom you are still married' and that becomes a kind of joke and later still watching a movie, she listens to a man and a woman in a kitchen talking, drinking warm strong black tea and the words she has spoken in what was to be the privacy of her sex are repeated in the film and far away the gears in the Maximum Leader's head turn with exacting slowness and he listens to Dick say we have broken their code, we will repeat their words on television and in films, and they will be drawn to the words and we will have them, and the former director of the ministry gives a speech in which he says, they use an elaborate literary code, and Mattya sits alone in her Spartan apartment and weeps as she feels her soul being raped and torn from her body as if it were to be cut again and again and again and staggering to her bookshelf, she begins to pull the books down tearing the pages out one after another.

✄✄

The Sultan's New Car

"You ask after the latest gossip...everyone is talking about the Sultan's new car—a British monstrosity with an enormous motor—and asking if his driver is a spy.... Of course those in the 'know' say that the story has been created by the Sultan's men in order to smoke out his enemies. Besides everyone knows he hates cars and only ever sits while his favorite mistress drives around the track while he watches and waves at her from the reviewing stand...it's the most sublime madness and really quite funny..."

— Lesharc A. Koffkalt
— Letters to Cavafy

✄✄

Henri Attends to Proust

"The pure present is an ungraspable advance of the past devouring the future. In truth, all sensation is already memory."

— Henri Bergson

૪ે ૨ે

You're Either with Us or Against Us

We met at the diner. It was open all night. There were televisions along the walls in the main back room. They were mounted on metal struts high up along the walls and they showed movies all night and all day.

We got a table near the front. We could hear the televisions but mostly it was quiet enough and there was only the blue flash from the screens that popped on the linoleum tiles of the floor.

I'd known him for years. He was a man of impeccable suburban credentials. He had a wife and two kids, a cat, a dog, a backyard, a sleek German sedan. He smoked excellent weed. We had been friends for years.

We sat in a booth next to the big tall window that gave us a view of the boulevard. The fog was rolling down the street. It came in wet cotton waves and the street lights lit the fog in squares of green yellow and red.

He ordered a burger fries and a diet soda. I ordered coffee and apple pie. While we waited we talked about baseball and who was the smelliest artist of all time. I said Caravaggio and he said Michelangelo.

The waitress brought our order and then he asked for another plate. She seemed confused and then she went and got another small plate and put it on the table.

He picked up a bottle of ketchup from the table next to ours and he squirted some onto his burger and fries and then he aimed the bottle at the empty plate. He moved it over the plate and he wrote: *I'm wearing a wire.*

He looked at me; I looked at him. His eyes were big and blue behind his glasses and his face was blank. He put the bottle down and took his burger and wiped the ketchup into a red formless smear. He bit the burger and looked at me.

—So, he said, how's the novel going?

—Great.

—Just what the world needs, he said exchanging his burger for his drink; another great verbal hulk full of allusions no one except dilapidated litchery monks will understand.

—Sure.

—You keep this up, you'll be a man without qualities.

—Would a man without qualities write a great verbal hulk?

—No, he'd just plan to write it and plan a party for it and never get around to doing it. And in the end he'll become an un-person.

—Great.

—So, he said, are you a Bolshevik?

I stared at him. He was working on his fries and washed them down with the soda. Then he went back to the burger.

—No, I said. I'm not.

—You sure? Sort of thing makes people curious.

—I'm not. Besides, I said, I'd make a rotten Bolshevik.

—Why's that?

—Same reason I make a rotten capitalist. I don't like being told which words I can use. Next thing you know, Uncle Joe is calling Boris Pasternak and asking about my purity.

—Would Pasternak rat you out?

—He didn't rat out Mandelstam.

—I thought he ended up in a gulag?

—Yes, but not because of Pasternak. At least not directly.

He stared at me; I stared at him. The fog came down the street. The floor flashed blue.

—Ever read Lenin on Tolstoy?

—No, he said.

—Like dancing to architecture.

He laughed and finished his food.

—Who said that?

—I don't know.

—Mencken, he said, Mencken said it.

—I don't know.

—Here's to Mencken.

—I don't know.

—See, he said, that's your problem.

—Yes?

—You read all that ex-pat Hemingway shit and you go limp.

—Really?

—Sure.

—I had no idea.

—There's a war on. People get nervous. They question your loyalty. Think you won't take it like man. They worry you'll get foreign ideas. Foreign ideas are limp ideas.

—Thanks for telling me.

—Don't mention it.

—What does one do then?

—Make a pilgrimage.

—To?

—Compostela.

—How do you get there?

—Oh, that's easy. The money can always be arranged.

—Especially in a foreign country.

He stared at me again. His face was blank. I got the pie to go and left the coffee. We paid and walked out to the street. It was cold and wet. I walked him to his car. He lit a cigarette and we walked without talking.

We got to the car and he opened the door and the interior light came on brightly white. He got in the car and the interior light changed to a soothing deep blue and the dashboard lights went on in shades of blue and red. He pressed a button and the window went down in a low buzz.

He looked at me.

—You ever read Heller?

—I saw the movie and read some.

—We just want you to like us.

—What?

—We just want you to like us. That's what they tell Yossarian. We just want you to like us.

He flicked his cigarette out to the street. It hissed in the thin layer of mist on the pavement.

He nodded and pressed a button and the window went up in a low buzz. He started the engine and rolled down the street. I watched him go and then he was gone and I walked home.

I opened the door when I got home and stood there for a moment and then closed it behind me and in the dark I felt the cats moving around me and

I stood there listening to myself breath and in the near-distance I heard the fog horn blowing. I was holding the bag with the apple pie in it. My hand started to shake and I stood there for a long time listening to the fog horn and then the telephone beeped twice, two short high-pitched tones for the tap on the line circling back on itself. I sat down on the floor and leaned against the wall and the cats came and sniffed the bag and then they sat down next to me and in the dark their eyes flashed dimly, half in shadow and then as small points of light.

ক্র

Brick

Audrey's father taught her how to shoot. She took Brick to the woods and shot tin cans that she had placed on top of an old wooden fence. The sound of the gun was the sound of the earth being torn open. She shot off an entire clip. She looked at me and then she loaded another clip and the air smelled of sulfur and there was blue-grey smoke and the cans were all shattered and then she took off her clothes and fired off the other clip and while she was pulling the trigger, the recoil made the skin of her ass quiver as the surface of a pool of water struck by a stone and she started moaning and then screamed yes,

yes yes, and when she was done she walked to the fence and bent over it.

ℰℛ

Crystal City

Guzman was renting office space in Crystal City. I used to know a studio guy who did public relations. He had an office in Crystal City. I used to have lunch with him from time to time. He paid. I ate well and he gave me the latest gossip. It was a good deal and once a month or so I'd drive out to meet him. Then the production company went bust when the bubble burst and he lost his job and I heard that he was out West fundraising and back when I knew him, I'd drive out there and watch the City being built—the vast interior of the then skeletal buildings and the way it was like watching a man being fashioned from dust, but not like that at all, and only metal and sheets of cardboard and drywall and wires that went on in dust or steel later to fade, and offices that would become coveted and marriages to be made in the offices to be built and marriages to be undone, jokes to be told at someone's expense, a flotilla of lies to be built in vast dry-docks full of very busy lawyers and words to fashion the lies imbedded as hot rivets turning cold... I remember when the doormen appeared at the condominiums, the Oxford Towers at Camden Place, as if in some Styrofoam super-collider you could ram home a dreamy never-was England into a vast open space full of *I want* or *I need* or as I called it, the Charlatan at the Next Place on the Map facing the plaza with the big faux imperial ruins motif done in a kind of Mussolini fascist chic with irony curving in every perfect stretch of marble as if the whole thing were already a footnote for itself, a gaudy theme park for bankers and real estate potentates pashas in suspenders and regimental ties and a legion of men their imaginations on permanent aggravated lockdown so that every idea they had was from the shelf of a store that sold ideas and inside each was the idea that each idea was unique and not from a store. It was like they had all purchased an identity and wore it and sent it to the dry-cleaners and then put in the closet until they needed it again. And inside the offices there were sentries stationed at large metal desks who smiled at you without meaning anything by it and their dull hungry eyes were always at parade-ready.

I rode up to a floor with a view of the city Alexandria splayed out in flat lines and low hills running towards the river and fabled Oz in the distance – the capital of the empire where they remembered everything and learned nothing.

I stood by the window and looked at it and after watching the unreal city for a while I went through a set of large wooden doors gave my name and best smile to the mannequin-receptionist at the front desk who pressed a button on a touch-pad on the desk, spoke softly into her boom-mike and commenced to ignore me and then another door opened and in walked Pepe Guzman extending a long arm and a long hand with big thick fingers and all of a sudden he stopped with a strange abruptness as if coming to attention before an unseen superior and he said in a crisp, accentless voice,

—Mr. Chandler, thank you for coming.

We sat in his office and he spoke into an intercom and told the mannequin-receptionist to hold all of his calls and he said as if reading from a script about a guy reading from a script,

—You must understand that we have reason to believe there is a leak from within this office. The story in the newspaper the other day exposing the government's wiretaps program was explicit and correct in many details and in one instance, they were right even if for the wrong reasons. It is true the government is listening to everyone including itself. It is true that they have blackmailed almost everyone and it is true that they have blackmailed the general because of his daughter just as he is blackmailing them by threatening to expose everything. Everything leaks eventually.

—As I explained, said Ray, the General hired me. I gave you the check, and you know as well as I do the bank went bust and the board of directors live elsewhere. No one could follow the details of the plot. You'd have to be some sort of savant to understand it. Besides in the end, everyone is guilty so who could you arrest?

—Yes, said Guzman, of course, but what matters is the name.

—I'll find the name.

—The name is what matters.

—You could have told me this over the phone.

—The phone is not secure. I've had the office taken care of. We play a decoy of our conversation. We pre-recorded it and play it and they think they are listening to us.

He waved his big hands in the air as if to suggest things being done vaguely, yet with a mysterious precision; and the look in his eyes said, with the inherent boredom of a man who is certain, that he is always the smartest person in the room, that this was beyond your pay-grade.

—And the leak?

—He'll come after you.

—That's why you invited me. You know he'll see me or someone will see me and tell him.

Guzman stared at me.

—It makes my life easier if you at least give me something to work with. In turn, it makes it easier for me to help you.

—The former special agent in charge of ambience in the west coast office, said Guzman.

—Was profiled in the Sunday magazine. He's your head of security.

Guzman smiled without meaning anything by it.

—He was brought in by the bosses, I said, to hide in plain sight. He has access to everything and can't be touched or asked any questions by anyone without forcing you to investigate them for asking the questions in the first place.

Guzman looked at his watch. It was a small elegant watch that seemed ironic at the base of his big hand.

—The name, said Guzman, the name is what matters.

—Sure, the name is what matters.

We said goodbye and Guzman was already turning the gears in the wind-up machine in his head and I was done, so I rode down without taking in the view a second time. It hadn't changed and I knew it hadn't changed and would never change except maybe where they had built the metro over the old slave market. I looked at the doormen in front of the Towers and the water gushing out of the fountain and the big Romanesque head on its side as if ruin and failure were already kitsch and the sunlight was very bright on the big glass windows of the buildings.

ᘉ ᘐ

The Story about their Mother

Mattya tells the story this way: She is at her kitchen table. She is wrapped in a red blanket. Her head is turning and her long black hair is fanned out, a tossed and beautiful mess of curls. She is naked under the blanket. Ariel is sitting across from her. They are both smoking. He is naked. She tells him about her mother. She says her mother was addicted to opium. She says they had to send her away to a clinic in Switzerland. He thinks about Switzerland and he thinks about a scarf and then she says that she and her ex-husband to whom she is still married were staying at her grandfather's house, the villa, when these men came.

—They wanted money, she said. My mother owed them money for the opium. They said it was not a problem. They said I had a week. They were polite. I had to sell some things. Old books. Her jewels.

He listened to her each word with a kind of practiced sincerity. Each word had resonance. Each word opened and closed as a small hand holding something large in its palm. He was listening and

238

writing. It was as if he were in a story. He looked at her. He was dripping out of her. Her lips were swollen. Her clit was sore. Tea was brewing on the stove. He knew then, that what she wanted was for him to see that she was embarrassed and that her embarrassment was a kind of suffering, which made her noble. He smiled at her. He listened to the tea brewing.

꙰꙰

Ariel

He is living in a safe house. There is a woman downstairs with two dogs. She drinks consistently and smokes many cigarettes. She never speaks to him. She watches him when he comes in and when he goes out and she records his schedule in a notebook.

Ariel has the attic room. It has a balcony that is unstable and slanted walls and one wall of exposed brick. It looks over a narrow street in the Old Quarter and out the back over the unstable deck, he sees the roofs and chimneys of other houses. Every day agents from the Ministry come to collect what he has written and to leave files for him to read.

Ariel is writing a novel. It is called The Love Song of J. Edgar Hoover. In the novel there is a character who the government listens to. They believe he is a terrorist. Later they believe he is a spy. Then they believe they were wrong, but by then it is too late. All he wants is to be left alone and to leave. By then they have dug an enormous hole and jumped into it and pulled everything down with them and sealed themselves inside the hole and eaten each other's eyes with rusty spoons. Sometimes they sing songs. Sometimes they make speeches.

In the morning Ariel drags a sharp knife over his wrists. He is trying to learn to endure the pain. He has put so much pressure on his tendons that typing has become painful. He smokes many cigarettes and he types and his wrists curl up and back as if they were held together by stale strands of rubber that had lost their elasticity and would soon snap leaving his hands to flap like the wings of a headless bird.

Ariel enjoys that image. He writes it into his novel. He writes about the detective from the Ministry who is being set-up to be a scapegoat. He writes about the new king who is being blackmailed by history. He writes about the old king who has the scent of an elephant at the moment of its death and the rabbit-headed general and the girl with the gun and the girl with the extraordinary hair who can see the past reflecting the future and he writes about the man who wrote the story that was stolen and made into many versions of the same story and how after years and days the ideas that had been stolen were generating copies of copies that were copies because nothing succeeds like success and the more he wrote the more he wanted to slit his wrists and one day all at once without effort the thought of killing himself brought a smile to his face and he observed the corner of his mouth curl up with unbidden joy.

✍ ✌

Tolstoy

A Brief Interlude in the Form of an Essay

Nikolai Chernyshevsky was a friend of Tolstoy's. Tolstoy thought Chernyshevsky was hot-tempered and intelligent. An extraordinary compliment when you think about it. And, of course, even when you don't.

Chernyshevsky wrote about his friend Tolstoy. He wrote: "...Tolstoy's attention is mostly aimed at how certain feelings and thoughts develop from others; he likes to observe how a feeling, coming directly from a certain situation or impression, obeying the influence of memories and the power of combinations, presented by the imagination, is transformed into other feelings, then how it returns to the original source and then again travels on, while changing throughout this chain of memories. Like a thought, born from a first experience, leads to other thoughts, getting carried away, further and further, mixing daydreams with real sensations, visions of the future with reflections of the present..."

Viktor Shklovsky, writing about Tolstoy: "Tolstoy spoke about linkages, a labyrinth of linkages – words don't stand on their own, they exist within the context of a phrase; a word juxtaposed to another word isn't an arbitrary word, it shifts the meaning into another dimension. It's a labyrinth of linkages that has a purpose."

Tolstoy describes the process of writing: *this* becomes *that* and *becoming* is a perpetual state; in this dimension of space-time-consciousness it is always *now* and we remember something called the *past*... if you ask a good writer why something happened, why for example, she loves him, instead of the other guy, you will cause a state of paradox in which on the one hand the writer will be paralyzed by the possibility of, as Tolstoy phrased it, selecting one possibility from the million possible combinations... and on the other, they will tell you well, she loves him because of the girl with the beautiful almost green eyes and their scintillating streaks of intelligent hazel... and because it was a Tuesday... and the café was open... and it was raining... and in Poland, in the winter, it is often very cold... and he will say that once again, the land fares ill full of some plague and it is exactly as predicted—it has all unfolded exactly as they said with the slow erosions of everything we believed we believed in.

❦

Tolstoy is a philosopher. He is also a scientist and he had a theory about labyrinthine linkages and he conducted a serious of experiments and among them are *Anna Karenina* and *War & Peace*. These are Grand Unified Theories of Everything.

They are applicable to contemporary politics but they are not only ignored, the very idea of their applicability is denied; ghettoized... exiled from the ideal city state...

At the end of *War & Peace*, Tolstoy lays out a post-Thuycidian, or neo-Thuycidian idea. History is the mass movement of people and from the surging tide an avatar rises who people mistakenly believe to be a leader of people and a director of events when in truth, the hand of god, present and yet invisible, moves all things; for when you connect the links that are the labyrinth, you find that where we draw a border, where we make the point of demarcation between this and that, between them and us, between this is how it happened and this is not how it happened, the edges blur, break down form new constellations and new linkages in an endless labyrinth that has neither beginning nor end and people, and ideas, and ideas that are people, are sub-atomic particles that are here and there, then and now; *potentia*... always becoming yet always repeating.

Anna, poor Saint Anna. She is always catching the train. And so, when someone says, 'I have a plan. Listen to me, I have a plan for making peace, here, there, between them and us,' I think of poor Anna, I even think of poor Saint Anna and I would laugh, were it not so awful, watching so many people march off the cliff.

ॐॐ

"...Moscow, about the back of your head..."

In Anna Karenina, Tolstoy was pushing the old world into its future. Or to put it another way, the new world used Tolstoy to drag itself into the present. It happens like this: Levin is at the theater with Kitty. He asks her what she is thinking. She says she is thinking about Moscow, about the back of his head. Tolstoy had freed himself from orthodoxy. He was asking his readers to join him in the present. In the present, the perpetual now that has no future and no past that can be touched except with sadness and awful joy, is always vanishing. Things that had always been described as separate were then smashed together in the great particle collision machine of Tolstoy's mind. Moscow and the back of Levin's head form a continent. A dream. A novel. Everything is connected. Nothing is alone.

☙

Mattya Writes a Story

Mattya is on television. She is on a talk show. Her novel has been published. Perhaps there will be a film. She is from a country that is often in the news and so she is considered very chic. She has little talent but she is not stupid and she is strikingly beautiful and her country is often in the news. Perhaps someday she will learn how to write. But for now what matters is everything else.

In her novel is a scene where a man vomits the truth. Many articles are written about this; about what a brilliant metaphor it is. It speaks to our times they say and it reveals a universal truth and her country is often in the news and that is very chic.

Just before he is retired, the chief of the Ministry makes a speech. He says 'we have proof of them working on elaborate cover stories and how they use an elaborate literary code to communicate'. No one asks him any questions about these theories.

But for now Mattya is on a talk show and the man after whom the show is named says, 'tell me about this book' and she lights a cigarette with a lovely flourish and her scarf is red and lovely and she talks about the book.

✆☜

At the Hemingway Museum

At the Hemingway Museum things keep falling apart... ideas... relationships... plans... honor... integrity... truth... Americans...

Patterns that revealed how themes repeated were displayed in such a way that gears of creation could be heard turning with all of the elegance of a Bach cello suite or a passage from the King James Bible...

There were advertisements as well... for virility and courage and beer and pens... and there were descriptions of fear and love and betrayal and there were other things as well... rivers and oceans and wide plains and the sky vast and true in its precise way and they endured...

At Caporetto there was a river of frozen mud. There were hills in the distance and beyond the hills were mountains. The mountains were grey. On top of the mountains there was snow brightly white in the sun. On the far side of the mountains were the Austrians. Then the Germans came and with them were many things from far away.

There was a glass case and in the case there was a reliquary. It contained fragments from an Austrian trench-mortar shell. Next to it was a photograph. In the photograph there was an ambulance on its side along the side of a road. In the ambulance there were men who had died. Beside the ambulance there were other men who stared at the camera. Later they would be dead as well.

J. Edgar Hoover came to the museum. He wore a disguise. He was pretending to be straight. It was a clever disguise and it worked well because no one believed it was Hoover. He was searching for clues. He sat in a room in a house in Oak Park where the lawns were wide and the minds were narrow and there was a sign that said: "My mother is an All-American bitch with handles."

In another room it was early in the morning and there was a sign that said Ketchum, Idaho. There were other rooms and they said Africa, Spain, France, Italy, Hunting, Fishing and Suicide. In another room there were many books and the books were a vast encyclopedia of every idea. J. Edgar walked around the rooms. He was still searching for clues.

J. Edgar had a list in his head. It was a list of everyone in the world. Each name was color-coordinated. Some names were in blue and some were in red and others were in pink. There were others in gray and sometimes the names changed places with each other. J. Edgar walked from one room to another and then he sat on a couch. Next to him sat Special Agent Automatic Turpentine.

The Ministry had many branches. Sometimes they ran universities. Sometimes they ran hospitals. Sometimes they ran countries. Sometimes they infected people with syphilis or gave radioactive food to children. Sometimes they sold drugs and killed the people they had paid to grow the drugs or ship the drugs and sometimes they ate each other's eyes. Sometimes they cut the hands from priests or blackmailed them into revealing the details of a confession. This was a sin and in heaven the list of sins was very long.

They sat on the couch and on the wall across from them, images came and went of Africa and Paris and Cuba.

—What, said Edgar, do you know?

—The General is getting old.

—He was born that way.

—Why is he the way that he is?

—He is the absurd symbol for an absurd idea.

—What idea is that?

—That we may control history.

—He is concerned.

—About?

—We paid him to pay men to rape nuns and cut their tongues from their mouths but now there is a problem.

Edgar stared at the images on the wall. One was of Marlene Dietrich. He was afraid of the image and closed his eyes until it went away and when he opened them he saw the image of a Cape Buffalo.

—What, said Edgar, is the problem?

—The nuns come every day to the main square in Xanadu where the local priest plays Russian Roulette and they stand there and they point.

—Point?

—Yes, they point, for hours at a time.

—At what do they point?

—They point at us.

—We are not there.

—Yes. But still, the General feels it is a problem.

—We have found a person of interest.

—Yes, said Turpentine.

—He understands the Super Atomic Piston Ring.

—Yes.

—We need to understand.

—Yes.

—We listen to his calls.

—Yes.

—We read his mail.

—Yes.

—We follow him.

—Yes.

—We arrest people he speaks with and make them informants.

—Yes.

—We isolate him.

—Yes.

—We threaten him.

—Yes.

—We tell everyone we are defending them.

—Yes.

—C is a problem.

—Yes.

—He refuses to choose sides.

—Yes.

—We must humiliate him or accident him to death or both.

—Yes.

—We must create a narrative that makes no sense and is elastic enough to accommodate every possible truth.

—Yes.

—We deny everything.

—Yes.

—We are responsible for nothing.

—Yes.

—We absolve ourselves of everything.

—Yes.

—When asked we recall nothing.

—Yes.

—This is the catechism.

—Yes.

—It is good, said Edgar, that no one listens and no one remembers.

—Yes.

On the wall a new image appeared. It was two men at a bar in Paris. There was a quote. It said: "History is a nightmare from which I am trying to awaken."

✄ ✄

Thomas Merton

Poor Thomas, he's still dead.

✄ ✄

F. Scott Fitzgerald

An Interlude in the Form of a Brief Essay.

"...so we beat on, boats against the current, borne ceaselessly into the past..."

Who has sufficient reason to say, that he is wrong? And if he is not wrong, what then shall we do?

✄ ✄

Audrey Goes

One day, I came home from the art store where I would go to buy paper and charcoal and when I got home, the house was empty and I found a note and Audrey said she needed to go away and she was gone and I stood there looking at the cats who sat there looking at me and all the blood and substance had leaked out of every object and the liquid substance had evaporated and left a thin film upon the floor and the chairs and the bed sheets and the silence was organic to the rooms and everything was like a clock that had lost its hands.

∅ ∅

Two Visions on the Street

I have nothing to do. I have nowhere to go. The phone never rings. No one ever speaks about anything except what they saw on television and the only other people who speak are informants who only ever repeat what I have already said.

I went for a walk in the park. I was crossing the street and I saw a car running over something bright and wet with rain from the day before.

I stopped and stood at the corner watching the traffic come and go in a steady pulse of exhaust and brakes and wheels churning up the puddles.

The cars stopped at the traffic light and the light was timed so the cars came and went in order and were predictable pistons of commerce and every car that went through the intersection ran over the thing wet and shining and then I looked closely and saw it well up as the cars went over it, saw it fall again as they left down the street and I saw it was a torn blow-up doll and that when the cars passed over it, the air shot inside making it rise at the waist and the doll face was cheerful and smiling with expectation; and when the car was gone, the air leaked out in a rush through a hole in the side of the doll and the air sounded as if it were going in a great breathing rush of life or exhaust or brakes and rain water and the doll rose and fell under the cars and I stood there on the corner watching it.

✑ ✒

Walking along, I saw a tangled grey and bloody mass in the middle of the street. It was a dead pigeon. One wing stood at attention, rising from the mass that had the tracks of a tire in it. A feather fluttered at the tip of the wing.

Another pigeon flew down from the roof of a house and landed near the mass. It circled it—its head snapping back and forth. It jumped up and flapped its wings and turned in a tight circle over the street and then landed on top of the bloody mass of meat and feathers and blood and something grey and flapped its wings rapidly and shot a load of pigeon jizz into the mass and stepped off and walked away down the street.

∅∅

Two Thugs Walk into a Bar

They came into the bar with their routine rehearsed. The Hispanic thug was back-slapping the White thug and making smiles telling him to loosen up and they walked into the bar with as much subtlety as a whale looking for a blow job in a cheap whorehouse. But luck was on their side as nearly everyone in the bar was brain-dead and on anti-depressants and wine and the music was loud. I was there waiting for a guy I knew who worked for the Ministry.

His name was Ryan and he did freelance work for the studio as a security consultant. 'It's simple,' he told me once. 'You see the bosses won't pay us enough to compete with the private sector, so they let us freelance. It's been going on so long now, you can't say who lives where anymore. We've gone borderless and country doesn't mean the same thing to us as it does to everyone else. In a country of lies, you don't need a passport'.

I waited for him at the bar and kept one eye on the two thugs. They were drinking vodka and tonic and the white guy was doing sullen while his pal worked on his clown routine trying to cheer up his sidekick. Ryan came in and pretended not to notice the other two, sat next to me and said hello.

He was about five-five with a steady tan and sandy blond hair. He was wearing a blue blazer, grey slacks, cuffed, oxblood loafers with tassels, a blue oxford button-down and a blue tie accented with gold stripes. He wore a class ring, a little smaller than a cape buffalo but less charming; and he ordered a beer and a glass of brandy in a snifter. When it came, he tilted the snifter over the top of his beer like he was making a modern art sculpture and then while we talked, he twirled the snifter around over the top of the beer using the beer glass as a tall thin cradle. It seemed to make him happy by which I mean, he focused on it and that made him calm, which seemed to make him happy.

—Listen Ray, he said, eye-balling the two thugs in the mirror back of the bar, someone hired you to step outside of your normal world. Normally, you'd be shut down right off, but the General has some pull even if he's gone soft in that fuzzy head of his.

—You giving me a warning?

—This is going to get ugly Ray. It's like that story you told me about where the guy sells his shadow and can't get it back.

—One of the lawyer's dogs slipped its leash and went for a walk.

—We know.

—You care?

Ryan thought about that. He stared at his contraption and slowly turned the snifter. The thugs were still working the sad Heckle and Jeckle routine. I waited and then Ryan smiled.

—I got a condo on the beach. I care about that. What helps make that real are the other things I care about. Ten years left until I get the full pension. But, I got some private contract work down south. Private investigations for a law firm handling divorce cases.

—You enjoy it?

He smiled again and looked in the mirror.

—Ray, he said, these two jokers aren't here for me.

—They won't do anything here. Twenty people in the bar. People know me here.

—Ray, take some advice—stick to fiction. Reality is dull.

—The lawyer won't let it go.

—Everything he says is in their office just as soon as he says it.

—You have the address for me?

Ryan worked on his drink and left a twenty on the bar. They went outside. It was warm out and the main street was full of a lazy drifting air and people walking slowly back and forth. There was a crowd outside of the ice cream parlor.

—Those two in the bar, said Ryan, I know them.

—Yeah, said Ray.

—Once, to make a point, they took this guy's kid. She was about three. Hit her in the head with a baseball bat. Then they soaked her in gasoline and dropped a match on her. Give it up Ray.

—The address?

Ryan looked down the street. The big red neon sign that said BANK was buzzing. A car with tinted windows rolled passed them and as it did, the driver's window slid down and the Hispanic thug gave me the dead-eye.

I winked at him and pointed my finger at him dropping my thumb like the hammer on a gun. The car went down the street and turned the corner and then it was gone.

—Be nice to see you again Ray, but I'm not going to count on it.

—Ye of little faith.

—Yeah, said Ryan, that's me.

—I'll take that address, I said.

—Sure, said Ryan, sure. You ever been to Mexico?

ℵ ℵ

Utta Pepe & the Magic Bullet

Ariel shot Utta in Mexico City. He shot her in the head, in Mexico City. There was a glass perched on top of her head and it must have fallen and shattered into many pieces, but I'm saying it was an apple. I like the apple idea better, but later we can try it with a glass. But first, the apple. William Tell and the apple. A woman and an apple. A *touch of evil* and Ariel becomes what he becomes and above all else, because hypocrisy is the truth of evil because it is the aborted fetus of evil and it slithers down your street leaving a trail of blood and semiotic fluid.

☠ ☠

Ariel is arrested because he is named and his voice is disembodied and heard on a telephone and his novel is discussed and later the government prosecutes him for dealing heroin while propping up gangsters who deal heroin. So, what did he do with the apple? Was it covered in blood and brain tissue? I want to believe, that he ate it. There would be something heroic in that.

☠ ☠

It is a new myth. Utta and the apple, the apple and Utta and Ariel and Utta and the gun and the apple turning in a buzzing, tumbling, red circle and brain and blood and bone and some of her hair all flying across space in a great shower of paralyzing, liberating emptiness.

Hang on to emptiness. Wear it with a grey fedora and a grey suit. What emerges from the myth is a legend. In Mexico City, heroin was inexpensive and not very good. Same as the boys, said Ariel, ruefully, same as the boys; and then he looked at his friend, and whistled a tune that sounded like something you might hear in a bar, in Kansas City, coming off an old juke box and for a buck, the bartender gives you a phone number and you call this guy who knows your name before you even say anything and you ask how he knows and he says it's always the same, it never changes and he says he'll send someone, so you wait in the bar thinking it's like waiting for a morgue to open.

෴

So, was the glass empty? Was it full? Who swept up the pieces? It was a party and there were people there; witnesses. Well not really a party, but still. Perhaps someone had a piece of the glass and kept it? Let's say that they did... it is a reliquary; and the dead saint is Saint Utta of the twin and what shall we say about her? She was no saint. She was just poor

Utta and she is a character in a story that has no beginning and will never end and she is always on her way to meet the bullet and she was an addict and she was in love with Ariel but his secret was queer and when they were about to have sex, he got a cramp in his foot. I guess it was easier and less embarrassing than going limp, and a cramp in the foot has such a nice mytho-poetic-literary referential quality, almost as if someone were writing a story. Yet, people believe. They believe in Saint Utta of the Shot Glass, the shot shot glass and Utta shot through the head and if you painted it and made her look like Saint Sebastian being shot with arrows, what would be the difference given enough time and the distillations of memory and faith?

☙❧

But it was not an apple. It was a glass; an empty glass and in one version of the story in the country of itself, in Mexico, no one ever mentioned William Tell and the bullet entered Utta's head but did not exit, but must have splintered and ricocheted around for a moment, some proverbial eternity of endless magic realism.

☙❧

Earlier there was the sound of a man playing a reed pipe. He was coming down the street to sharpen knives. It's an old established custom—a man on a bike with a whetstone to sharpen your knife. Ariel had a knife. He had purchased it in the south, in Central America, while searching for god, or himself and he was there and perhaps he was in love or not and he is standing on the street with the knife and he hands it over to the man with the reed pipe and the whet-stone and he is overcome with a devastating sadness. Later, thinking about the knife and the sadness, he aims the gun at the wreckage that is Utta and the truth and there is a magic bullet that enters but never leaves and a glass that is an apple that never shatters, but contains all knowledge of how things are the way that they are.

ꝒꝬ

The Broken Glass

Ariel's parents' neighbors were a couple with three kids and the father was a union organizer and Ariel's mother was an informant for the Ministry. Every morning she fell out of bed and broke on the floor and had to piece herself back together again.

ꝒꝬ

Many years later, further along in the story and before another part of the story that occurs later, they went on a trip to Idaho and one night at an ice-skating rink his mother met a man. He sat at the table and they spoke. He was very well-dressed and very thin. His father was from the area and was soon to be dead from cancer so the elegant man said he would meet with the woman even though she was no one and he was responsible for counter-intelligence for the Ministry.

He said, 'You should enter the boy in summer camp when he turns nine. We believe these summer camps are being used to recruit people to work for someone else and once he is in the camp, you will meet the parents and tell us about them. The most fantastic things are just as likely to be true as those that are most obvious. But of course no one believes in such things.

✂ ✄

In the story as Ariel tells it, his mother walks into a bar in Kansas City and sounds like an old tune from a juke box and she walks up to the old queen at the bar whose face looks like the inside of a morgue and she says let's go, and he has the urge to stab out his eyes.

So they go out the back and down an alley and she gives him an envelope full of small bugs that dance and then, they form a needle and inside the needle there is bug blood and Ariel shoots up right there and after a while he looks at her and says, 'you're a fragile glass, aren't you?' and she laughs nervously and then a little more and soon she can't stop and starts cracking into thin lines running up her arms and across her face and Ariel says, 'Christ I thought *I* had it bad,' and then just sort of falls into pieces—a big pile of jagged little shards that reflect the dim neon lights in shaking pulsing shades and shafts of blue and red and green—and then on long thin crab legs, she starts to move sideways down the alley clicking her claws in tune to the music, slipping out of the bar... And people find this to be very mysterious, but this is the story as Ariel writes it and sometimes you get gulags and sometimes you get *Born to Run* and no one can say why.

☙

Amid the wreckage of Utta were shards of glass. They have had flecks of blood on them. There are pieces of brain matter, skin and hair. Perhaps there was an apple.

To avoid prison, Ariel's parents paid a lawyer twenty thousand dollars and he used that money to pay people bribes to avoid going to prison. This is how things work. The cops are full of criminals and the judge goes to a local whorehouse that specializes in children and when someone refuses to pay a bonus the whole story suddenly, mysteriously, magically ends up all over the news.

Instead of prison he left the country. He went to France. Once in France, he began dealing heroin. He got caught. The French government had decided to shut down the heroin trade in the South and Ariel was caught up in that and the heroin dealers relocated to Mexico.

The great bladder of commerce, the great talking sphincter of trade created the exchange in which Ariel left Mexico for France and in his place the heroin left France for Mexico and there, amid the wreckage that was Utta, it set up shop and settled in for a long generational stay.

∅ ∾

Ideas of Escape

In the kitchen of a restaurant amid the hum-whir of dishwashing machines and the whir-humming of men and women, a waiter hands me a plate and from under the paper under a shrimp, a little smaller than Texas, I pull a matchbook with an address on it.

☙ ❧

A relatively small, red, neon sign flashed in the right lower corner of the window in a small beach house: *Exit*, and made a red splash on the mist-wet gray sidewalk.

I rang the buzzer on the metal gate there, at the foot of the wooden steps, once long, and twice, short; and after a few minutes, an old German Pointer shuffled down, its nails like a slow typewriter in use clicking loudly.

Behind the dog, came a man who wasn't old but looked it; his eyes a little sunk and his face worn out with some wasting disease and his clothes hanging oversized and too loosely on the too thin frame beneath. The small red light of a cigarette went up and down in his mouth smiling as he came closer as we knew each other from the neighborhood and he opened the gate, and the old dog sniffed and I said hello and Jo Knife, which was his real name, smiled and we all three went upstairs to the living room of the old beach house and it was dark but warm and not uncomfortable.

—Well, you know, he said, with the dog on a shabby couch, I was away for a while, he said, and it's cool, you know, I had my ride, and then did the time and it was alright.

He never said anything about being away and

told the story about being sold out and having to go away deeper and longer and darker from *some time* to *hard time*. We spoke about his dog and getting older and how there were two of us who wanted Orders for Transit, which he called a magic carpet for two and two cats and that was all, and he said he'd be in touch and 'Audrey and I met at a café as if in Night Hawks or Night Cafe, Arles,' with the morgue yellow-white lights of the interior falling upon us and the sad girl in the stocking cap leaning on the counter examining her tattoos, and the one man in the back, cheerlessly looking over test papers and then the streetcar rumbling and clanking by at the end of its run, empty except for the driver, showered in the yellow light of the coach's interior, the overhead wires igniting moistly in the sea-mist in a brief popping-loud cum-shot of blue and blue-purple and red sparks; and we did not speak of it but only went home and went to bed.

☙ ❧

But no one goes anywhere. Days pass and weeks and people who were eager to know you become anxious and fearful and eventually they stop answering the phone and when you ask if anyone has seen them lately, you just get a blank stare as if they never existed and then one day you realize that you are the one who had disappeared and no one remembers you and no one can say if you were tall or short. Then you see someone you knew once who you haven't seen in years, one of those who had vanished for a long time and all of a sudden they keep showing up seemingly at random and they come right at you with this overly-expansive jagged friendliness and they start asking you where you are going and with whom and it keeps happening like that until you know you are being followed and you get so angry, you want to expose them somehow so you speak loudly in a crowd crossing the street about being followed by an informant and no one says anything, no one looks at you except the person you once knew and they stare at you with a face that seems ready to crack, eyes all wide and full of desperation and they plead with you to stop but there are no words, only the face that seems to be vibrating and ready to go to pieces.

So you imagine plaster falling off a façade and all of this happens as you are crossing a street or passing through a crowd at the subway station; it all happens in a few seconds that last forever and you walk one way and the informant walks the other and they turn away into the crowd.

You will remember the fragility of their face and you will imagine how they bought weed from a cop by mistake or had been caught with sellable weight or holding cash for someone who had a bag of pills or they were cheating on a spouse and the cops went through their trash and found something to blackmail them with and you imagine how they were given a choice to snitch or go away down deep and forever and this knowledge expands like a slow, rolling fog as you see one after another of them drifting across the whole of the world, an army of informants seeding the earth with moldy spoors compelled to give information about the banality of every day life until every detail becomes a sinister bend of the truth.

So you feel yourself drifting into Chandler-town; shabby town, crooked town full of furtive faces and men with unexplained limps and awful breath; people who seem to twitch as if they know their going to get hit; people who always ask the same questions about where you've been and where you're going? and who's that you were talking to and how is that novel coming along and do you need anything— weed shit pills boys girls money prescriptions favors, and they come looking for you as soon as you leave your house and somehow they know just where to find you and eventually with all the surprise of the street-lights changing colors, they beg you to hold a bag for them just for a little while and you stand there on the edge of the truth and the abyss and you say, no I can't help you and you walk away and the look in their eyes is desperate starving hysterical, knowing there will be no salvation.

But then you cross the bridge in the other direction and you think of the wreckage you leave behind: the overpriced too-small apartments, the junkies passed out in the hall, the sloppy drunks, the people who work with their hands, the people waiting in lines for service that will be rude at best, non-existent at worst, and you go amid the splendor of wide lawns and quiet streets where the traffic lights never go out and you find it's exactly the same, only the prescription pills are better and more easily obtained and the doctor is his own best customer and people in nice clothes ask you where you've been and with whom and their faces are elegantly appointed immobile walls behind which someone is weeping in perpetuity and despair and when you are alone they ask you to do them a favor—will you deliver a package an envelope? will you hold a bag for them just for a while? and they smile, but the smile never reaches their worn-out eyes. Instead it hangs there frozen.

So you have stark moments of self-awareness, realizing in an ugly flash of emotional tungsten that you live there too, you are the worn-out face standing in front of a seedy bar like the worst sort of cliché and you are the one talking to the derelicts crashed on the hidden reefs, the homeless and fractured transvestites debating the spiritual degeneracy of their customers, the drunks and the dealers; and across the bridge, you are the one listening to the blackmailed executives and their tricked-out trophy wives at some dead-on-arrival party where they serve whispers and poisoned gossip alongside the *pâté,* then one day you watch some almost-famous poet step out of the old bookstore where they still sell pocket-editions of *Howl* and you see some robot in the uniform of a tourist so obviously not a tourist, raise a camera and start firing off images of the man in the doorway of the bookstore and you know he's being watched and no one says anything, no one does anything and this is where you live and this is who you are in the unreal city where fear has undone so many and no one believes you, and later when it's been revealed that they are listening to everyone, no one cares and a man with unwavering eyes and a steel face finds you at a store or a café and watches you, just stands there and stares at you and follows you to the bus stop, gets on the bus with you, gets off where you do and walks along the other side of the street staring at you and stops and stares as you walk in your front door and you know you are become a slave in a rainy kingdom of fear. So you know this is how it goes and it's at one of those parties that someone makes an introduction for you and you meet a man with a smile like polished chrome and a face like an advertisement for the side effects of selling out and climbing the ladder. Then when he tells you his name, you half laugh and you can't help yourself and for a moment, but only a moment, you feel bad.

—Cheever Stoodley? That, I said, sounds made up.

He smiles his winning smile. He holds his drink and gazes at you with steady blue eyes and an immobile air of calm certainty that he is always right about everything.

—That's alright, I'm used to it, he says. Besides, if you wait long enough, everything sounds like it's been made up. After all, look at the Crusades. Who believes that was real?

He gives you his card and you stand there for another of those seconds that seems to pull you along for an hour and then it collapses in on itself and you listen to him repeat fragments of things you've said in what was supposed to be the privacy of your home and you know someone somewhere wants to arrange a conversation.

A week goes by and you stare at the card and it hums and vibrates even though it does nothing at all and then you call him. Of course he'll be happy to meet you; why not come to his office?

⌀·⌀

West Berlin, Alexanderplatz, November, 1989

An East German soldier, in a forest green winter jumpsuit stands atop the wall, holds his automatic rifle in his gloved hands, and stares forlornly at the crowd on the other side.

☒ ☒

West Berlin, a rented furnished room, above the Kurfurstandam, November, 1989

In our rented room the radio announcer says that the American Senator from Massachusetts is in West Berlin. The night before, perhaps two, it snowed. The street is clear and great piles of snow are standing on the curbs and the memorial to the wall in which two enormous backsides of two enormous American cars from the late 1950s are pointed skyward protruding from a massive block of cement, covered with precise squares of snow.

She is very happy. She says, she whispers, that she has family on the other side. She has not seen them for years. I ask about them. She tries to deflect my questions with smiles and with her joy, but I persist and eventually she gives up names, ages, professions. Her grandfather. Yes. Him. No, yes, perhaps, no one knows; no one talks about it.

She says, sometimes, he takes his uniform out from the back of the closet and puts it on and if no one catches him, he goes outside and walks up and down the street. Once, they found him in a bar sitting, drinking a beer. The bartender called them and said, 'You have to come right away and collect him; he's making everyone nervous.'

The Warrant Expires

One day, I said to Audrey, 'I read an article that said they issue these emergency warrants. The Ministry issues them and they can do as they please for a period of time. But if you don't talk, if they have a tap on your phone and you don't talk or if you only communicate using sign language, or you just write everything down they have nothing to listen to.'

She thought about it and we stopped talking at home. We wrote notes. We made gestures. We had sex in silence. Our cats stopped meowing. We went on like that for three months.

The silence became someone. It had a personality that was everything in the apartment and yet it was nowhere and principal or agent, it could not be sought out but arrived as a whale might arrive, more massive and heavy than could be understood, and yet able to vanish to a point no bigger than the fingerprint of your soul. Sometimes it was three in the morning and it was the one light you turned on in the silence in the room while in another room, men from the Ministry sat in silence and listened to the silence in your room and grew angry until their anger grew as big as the fingerprint of any whale.

Then, at midnight on the last day of the third month, a few minutes after turning off the light in the bed room and going to sleep, we heard someone moving on the roof above our apartment. We lived on the top floor; our ceiling was the underside of the roof. We could hear the steps distinctly.

We heard two sets of feet. Then, they started jumping up and down, stomping with heavy boots and making the roof shake and the light fixture in the ceiling sway and rattle. Then they ran from the roof and Audrey ran to the window and said she could see them—two of them running for a car. They got in the car and soon they were gone, going fast down the street and you felt sick in your stomach and your chest was tight, your heart beat in your throat and you could not stop your hands from shaking.

☙❧

Television

In country of the novel there is a television show. In it a mysterious stranger who is also a troubled handsome young man arrives in a wealthy town by the sea. The show is ruthlessly hip. There is music from new bands played on the show and the company owns the musicians and owns the show and sucks the leprous cocks of the advertisers who place ads on and in the show and in-between the show. They make money as people come into the tent past the sign that says enter, and again as they leave the tent past the sign that says exit, smiling cheerfully as one hand diddles them and the other reaches for their wallet.

I'm watching the show. The character, the mysterious and troubled young man, is talking to the beautiful girl who is the daughter of the wealthy family that has taken the young man in to save him and give him a second chance.

He tells her about living on a Greek island. He tells her about how his girlfriend almost died because of an accident. Something involving a rock and a steep hill. A woman who only ever whispers. He tells her about meeting a man who swears he is being followed.

He says one day, he was sitting outside the courthouse in Athens and he saw a dead pigeon in the street. He was waiting for his lawyer. His lawyer was talking to the judge and another lawyer. There was going to be an arrangement.

The lighting in the show is exquisite. The actors are all terribly attractive. There is a swimming pool and the light reflects off the very blue water and the shadows are delicate and languid. He tells her about the pigeon and then he describes how this other pigeon came and went and it's all very moody and mysterious and dramatic and the show was an enormous success until suddenly, it wasn't.

Later within the within of the television show, there is a story about a character who is a character in a television show. He is the son of a lawyer who lived in Georgia a long time ago. He tells a story about his father and a preacher and the story is called *The Door to God's House* and in the story the preacher who is named Parting Waters laid a dead child down into a white cloth on a table in the kitchen of the small house, sprinkled water on the child's forehead and made the sign of the cross and no one knows that the preacher is an informant for the police and he knows that the man who killed the girl is an informant and that if he ever went on trial for his crime he would expose all of the informants and the police said to the preacher you can never tell anyone the truth.

The show was an enormous success. Many people spoke about it and it was given many awards and I watched a talk show and listened to the man who they said had written the show and said he wanted to write a second show in which the first show appears on the televisions of the characters in the second show because he said it would convey the reality of how we live and I watched the program and my apartment was empty and still and then the man who lived next door and who believed people were coming out of the telephone, started screaming.

☙ ❧

Cheever Stoodley's office was on the seventeenth floor. I went there on a Friday morning. The secretary was pleasant and distant and let me wait for a few minutes in a comfortable room and then Cheever came in radiating good health and sporting a fresh tan from around his casual uniform of jeans and sailing shoes and in the middle of his pale sweatshirt was a crest for the Ministry of Ambiance's legal department. It showed a knight, kneeling and holding a sword. Around the crest were the words: '*The truth seldom has anything to do with the facts.*'

We shook hands and he brought me into his office. It was the corner office and the entire far wall across from the door was glass. The view was of the bay and the East Bridge and the waterfront. Threads of fog drifted by at eye level. He offered me a seat across from his desk and he sat down and put his legs up across the corner of the desk and smiled, lacing his big hands behind his head. Cheever Stoodley, lawyer. Arbiter of god's will.

Behind him on the wall, alongside his diploma and various awards from various legal societies, were many photographs that showed important moments within the world of Stoodley, including him shaking hands with the president and shaking hands with the Secretary of this and the Secretary of that and another of him standing along side the chief of the Ministry.

—So, he said, what can I do for you?

I looked at him and ticked off the details of his personality and as I did, something inside me came to the fore. It was a feeling of detachment and it was familiar from every other time I had spoken with someone who possessed the oily residue of having been in the septic tank and from whom came the odor of decay blended with the genuine sense of faith that they were involved in a great adventure and that the shadow that was cast by the rancid mountain of skulls upon which their fortune had been built, was not at all some dark babble-tower but was instead a perch from which one might watch an entertainment provided just for your pleasure.

—Well, I said, as I mentioned at the party–

—Jim's party?

—Yes.

—How do you know him?

—From the neighborhood. He owns the car dealership and we have friends in common and–

—Yes, he said, you had a hypothetical question.

He kept up the smile and then came forward in his chair, bringing his hands from behind his head and resting them on his chest. The questions and comments were a distraction, a lawyer-trick to swerve and pivot and establish a moment of power where none was needed. I smiled.

—Hypothetically, I said, let's say there was a tap on your phone.

—Okay, he said, let's say hypothetically, there was.

—And, I said, let's say the sort of people, government people, who put a tap on your phone, decided you were doing something dangerous.

—Okay, he said, why would they think that?

—Let's say, it was because somewhere along the way, you knew someone who knew someone who knew people who were doing something dangerous but—

—But what?

—But the people who were doing the dangerous thing were doing it with money and tools provided by people who work alongside the people who placed the tap on your phone.

—That, said Cheever, would be a funny sort of thing.

—Yes.

—Go on. He smiled encouragingly.

—Well, to complicate things, let's say that the person with the tap on their phone knew they were being listened to and when they went out of their house, they ran into people–

—People?

—The sort of people who put a tap on your phone and who, it turned out, had not learned any new tricks in say, nearly fifty years and after decades of books and movies and television shows about those sorts of people often written with the assistance and guidance of people who had retired from say, a government agency, had made the entire arsenal of tricks, banal. Obvious.

—Hmm, said Cheever, I haven't heard of that being a problem.

—What was the last book you read?

—A biography of Cotton Mather.

—I just finished a biography of Hemingway. He was being spied on.

—Says?

—His government file.

—Okay.

—So, how many people do you know who read anymore?

—Hardly anyone.

—So, let's say you were going about your business and these people kept showing up every time you went out and they spoke to you and they just happened to repeat things you had said in your home to a friend.

—Coincidence, said Cheever.

—Right, I said, the first ten times. But after that, in order to test yourself, let's say you said something to a friend, in private, in your home, and it was a kind of breadcrumb, a special sort of breadcrumb.

—What would make it special?

—Let's say it was split into two parts. Part one was a true, but obscure literary reference.

—And the other?

—A false statement about the previously mentioned literary item.

—Like?

—Like Jake Barnes was ineffective and secretly in love with Gatsby.

—Was he?

—They never met.

—Go on.

—Well, if you say that and then you go out and someone you don't know strikes up a conversation and they have a copy of say, Gatsby, and they look at you with big searching eyes and a kind of desperate air about them and then they say, 'It's funny about Jake and Jay.'

He stared at me. I stared at him.

—Do you, he said, believe in conspiracies?

—Oh, I said, that ploy. You mean do I believe

there was a plot to kill Caesar or Napoleon or Lincoln or Roosevelt, or Yamamoto, or Hitler, or–

He laughed. It seemed genuine. He looked away. His cell phone lit up and he stared at it and then he looked back at me.

—Okay, he said. Maybe you just attract odd literary types.

—Sure, except it happens like clockwork. I say something odd to a friend, in my home, and every time I go out–

—Well, said Cheever, there is a war.

—So?

—So there's a war.

—And, I said, let's say hypothetically, you were the sort of person who kept running circles around the people who put the tap on your phone and they got angry and mistakenly believed you were some sort of a professional and if you weren't, you should be and if you were going to be, then you should work for them.

—Would that, he said, be so bad.

It wasn't really a question. He was not smiling. He was serious. He stared at me. I stared at him and then I looked out the window. The bridge was a long dull gray line that arched over the brightly blue water of the bay. On one side of the bridge there was a layer of thick fog hanging above the water and on the other there was just the long bright stretch of the waves rising and falling brightly blue caped with foam. I looked back at him.

—I don't see any daylight between one side or the other.

—You don't?

—Who pays their salary?

He smiled. He rocked back a little in his chair and placed his hands on the desk as he came forwards.

—So, he said, hypothetically, a tap is on someone's phone, who it seems, is smarter than the people listening, and through a bit of hyper-intellectual sleight of hand has succeeded in confounding and making angry a lot of people.

—Hypothetically.

—Well, said Cheever, that would pose an interesting challenge. What would such a person do to extricate themselves from what could be an otherwise eternal Kafkaesque limbo?

—You, I said, tell me.

—If it were me, he said, I'd make a deal.

—What sort of a deal?

—Let's say the person who was confounding the people who placed the tap, were to explain themselves.

—You mean the rape victim should justify the rapists.

—That, said Cheever, is one way of looking at it.

—And another?

—There's a war on. Makes people nervous.

—There's always a war on. Saying there's a war is like saying, there's weather.

He laughed.

—That, he said, sounds pretty hardboiled to me.

—So?

—So, he said, let's go downstairs and get some coffee.

He didn't wait for an answer and I followed him out of the office and we went down to the street to a café.

After we had bought our coffee we sat at a table and he said:

—You know, I worked for the Ministry? It's sort of an umbrella for all the rest.

I said nothing. He turned his coffee cup in his hands. The café was quiet. There was a man sitting at a table. He was looking at his computer. A woman worked behind the counter cleaning a large coffee press.

—The current boss, Cheever went on, got his job because a senator wanted him to have it. He has a reputation for being sloppy.

—The senator?

—No, she's competent enough, for a senator, but the current boss. He's being held over.

—Is that unusual?

—Yes.

—Why is he being held over?

Cheever raised his cup and looked at me over the rim as he sipped his coffee.

—Because as long as he's inside, he can't be sued.

—Oh. For what would he be sued?

—Using the Bill of Rights as toilet paper. For believing it's just a piece of paper.

—Oh.

—Yes, well, let me ask you a question.

—Sure.

—Ever hear of Lazar Katzenberg?

—Yes.

—What have you heard?

—He's a fictional character in a book by some shrink who had a crazy patient who insisted they were being spied on by the government and Bess Truman.

—Bess Truman?

—Yes, Harry's daughter.

—My, you wouldn't want that.

—No, I guess not.

—Suppose, said Cheever, Lazar was real.

—Okay.

—Suppose someone had figured out, that not only does everything repeat, but that you could explain, and predict, just how everything would repeat. That you could listen to every conversation in the world.

—Christ, I said, what's next? Every time you have sex, a German rocket explodes over your head?

He stared at me.

—It's from a book.

—Well, he said, you see, there you go.

—Where do I go?

—Figuring things out.

—So?

—Imagine explaining to people, certain people, how things happen.

—I don't want to work for anyone.

He turned his coffee cup again and stared at the contents.

—Do you think we're going to win the war?

—No.

—Why not?

—I saw some professional gasbag the other day, a pasha from some part of the regime. He was explaining that the bad guys were on the ropes and were, as he put it, hard up for cash.

—So? Maybe they are.

—Oh, I don't doubt it, but what struck me was, so are we. We're broke. We've lost. We did exactly what they wanted us to do.

He looked up from his cup and smiled.

—And what, he said, do you think will happen?

—What always happens, I said. Coup, counter-coup, repression, justification, terror, over-reach, cover-ups, crimes, bankruptcy, collapse. Like the Peruzzi and the Bardi loaning money to the King of England so he could beat up the French and neither winning nor losing and going broke and not paying his debt and the debt having been sliced and repackaged at interest sort of metastasized and while not the proximate cause, well, it certainly didn't help and then—it's all toxic.

I smiled at him and he stared at me and he looked quizzically at me.

—They went bust, I said, they keep going bust, and when they do it's like one of those cartoons where someone buys an ACME rocket and it blows up in their face and right before they collapse into a pile of burnt-out dust, they blink at you with an expression of utter confusion and defeat.

—That keeps happening?

—Yes.

—Why not explain it? That's the sort of thing people might be inclined to pay for. Explaining what would happen next after you listened to recordings of people talking.

—I'm not for sale.

He sat back in his chair.

—Well, he said, then hypothetically speaking, what do you think will happen as the empire collapses into a pile of burnt-out dust?

—Everyone will be in the same boat.

—No, he said. There will be the ones who are a pile of burnt-out dust and the ones who aren't.

We sat there and the seconds were thick and long and then they weren't and we were outside and he was smiling and then he stopped near the corner and whistled a tune I didn't know.

—Perhaps, he said, I could make a call.

—Why bother, I said.

—It might prove useful.

—I won't hold my breath.

—You know, he said, be a shame to let a golden opportunity slip away.

I looked around and we watched a bus go by and sparks shot off from the overhead wires above the bus. They made a loud crackling noise like a plastic bag being popped and the sparks shot out in short sharp blue splashes.

—I just want to go away, I said.

—No such place, said Cheever, no such place.

He shook my hand and he walked away saying over his shoulder he'd call and let me know. I didn't answer him.

A week later he left a message on my voicemail. It was jaunty. He said he had nothing to tell me. That was the last time I heard from him. The following Sunday I saw him on television. It was a news show, called Fifty Minutes. He was being profiled. He'd won a judgment in a law suit. It was a glowing profile.

☒ ☒

Heroin & Cars

The drug trade, Ariel wrote, is the perfect metaphor in the contemporary landscape. He said, the car you purchase today is an improvised explosive device next week. Follow the money, follow the drugs, follow the food. A grain of rice is god. God is a grain of rice. In the spring there is a harvest. The crop is food and money and opium and power and the king of Xanadu had an elaborate crown and in one part of the crown there were golden poppies and in another the sun and between them was a river from which the mind of god flowed into the body of the king.

Then there was a revolution. The men from the Ministry who had helped the king to sit on his throne came and the king was taken away and was encased in amber in a crate made from amber and was sent far away and the people who had been tortured by the men from the Ministry became the people who ran Xanadu and the Men from the Ministry said, 'We will provide advisors,' and there were people who carried small pieces of amber in the shape of a crate everywhere they went and it was as if a great wind had blown them across the earth and they were scattered as seed pods into the soil of what we call history and if you asked them what the amber was, they would sigh deeply and forlornly saying it was a grain of rice and then they would light a cigarette with a great dramatic and sad flourish that covered up the true sadness of remembering. Then they drank many cups of strong black tea and often listened to sad, romantic music staying up very late and sleeping in very late and things kept happening but nothing ever changed and everyone remembered and no one forgot and no one learned anything and everyone waited for the story to start again.

ᛟᛞ

Ketchum, Idaho 1961

He could smell them. He could not see them at first, but he had seen their shadows. Three nights before, he had heard them.

At the diner, near Butte, he saw one cross the road. No one believed him. But he knew a hyena when he saw one.

Two men were in a booth in the diner. They were

sitting so they could watch the door. It was Sunday. The men were in dark suits with white shirts and thin dark ties. He asked the waitress if she knew them. She said they were insurance salesmen.

"Insurance salesmen don't work on Sundays," he said.

She poured coffee for him into the plain white mug on the table. He drank the coffee. He ordered ham and eggs with toast. Outside the road was empty and then a logging truck went by and he counted the number of dead trees on the bed of the truck.

☙ ❧

He was thinking about Cuba. He sold his own manuscripts. He penciled notes in the margins. The buyers liked that. He always gave the broker a good cut. It was all always cash.

The broker owned a taxidermist shop. It was down at the end of a narrow alley. On one corner was a good café and at the other was a bait shop.

He liked the taxidermist. He did good work. But now he was having trouble.

—There's extra cops at the port, Hem. In the Keys. You know when you're being watched.

—Don't worry. We'll be alright.

—I'm sorry. Last time they followed me, I'm certain

of it.

—Nothing to be sorry about. You're not responsible for the rotten weather.

—Still, I'm sorry Hem. I said I would do it. But I can't. Too many cops. They waited for me at the hotel.

—It's alright.

—Why do they give everyone so much trouble?

—Fear.

—Fear? Their fear or ours?

—Both.

—I'm sorry. I was unable to help you.

—It's alright.

—Drink?

—Sure.

They drank rum. It was warm and sweet. On the walls were the heads of many dead animals.

☙☙

He could smell them. They were close. They did not care if he knew. The mail was being intercepted. The phones were no good. There were stories he still wanted to write, but he could no longer remember the details. He heard one of them moving on the front porch. It was sniffing the wood looking for the scent. He went downstairs and turned on the porchlight. He looked outside and there were fireflies drifting in the summer air. He turned off the light. He sat on the couch. It was early in the morning.

☙❧

Kaddish

"Decades later... the F.B.I. released its Hemingway file. It revealed that beginning in the 1940s J. Edgar Hoover had placed Ernest under surveillance because he was suspicious of Ernest's activities in Cuba. Over the years agents filed reports on him and tapped his phones. The surveillance continued through his confinement at St. Mary's Hospital. It is likely that the phone outside his room was tapped after all."

— A.E. Hotchner

☙❧

The Princess & the Detective

She looked like the best idea god could have had that day and she knew it. She was wearing black the way a leopard wears fur and she was so sure of herself that when she came in to the bar she did not stop to adjust to the dark and she did not stop to see if anyone was looking at her, nor did she stop as everyone else did to check her look in the big mirror on the wall at the top of the stairs.

She came down the stairs like water came in to an empty pool and everyone watched her as if they had been thirsty for a long time.

—Raymond, she said, it is good to see you again.

Ray stood and helped her with her coat. She let him. She sat and smiled. It was the low wattage one; she saved the full one for causing blindness. Ray motioned to the bartender. She ordered a gimlet.

—So, she said, do you always meet your clients in a bar?

—I consider it a kind of home-field advantage.

—How quaint.

The waiter brought the drink. She ignored him. He went away. She ignored her drink. She looked at Ray. He looked at her.

—When did you know?

—The first time we met, he said.

—What was it?

—Utta couldn't be in two places at the same time. You never lost the ticket.

—But the ticket was stamped.

—I didn't know that until just now, he said.

She sat back as if he had pushed her. The color went from her face. Nothing they were saying made any sense. Her eyes grew big, then small. She laughed to buy time. She waited, then she put her hands around her glass.

—This is a cliché Raymond. Clichés are for amateurs.

—Nothing is original. Besides as you well know good artists copy, great artists steal.

—My mother's husband is paying you.

—The money is in an envelope in my apartment, said Ray. I'll return it.

—I'll pay you.

—I don't want your money.

—It's just a story, said Mattya. It's just a story. Why can't you just see that it's a just a story?

—No, said Ray, it's the truth.

—The truth, she said in a hiss. The truth is a story everyone agrees on. It's all his fault. Ariel is to blame. He stole the story. He's betrayed all of us.

—And your sister took the name from the list, and gave it to the senator.

—Do you have it? Give it to me Ray. Give me the name before they find him.

—C. wrote those stories.

—He's nothing. You know they are tight with money. We're different Ray. Help me and I can help you.

She leaned across the table. Her eyes were sharply focused. She opened her mouth a little and her breath became deep and slow.

—Raymond, listen to me, she said and she put her

hands out on the table. Guzman is a liar.

—He's a lawyer, said Ray. The surprise would be if he weren't a liar.

—Oh Raymond, your cynicism is charming. You charm me Raymond. I have money. My stepfather has provided for me.

—So to speak.

—Don't be vulgar. It's not becoming.

—There are places you can go.

—Go? What do you mean go? What places Raymond? Don't tease me.

Ray looked at her. She smiled. It was the full one. She was beautiful. Ray stared at her.

—There are places where they can't or won't extradite you, he said. You can avoid giving testimony. But it won't matter.

—Oh Raymond, it's so ridiculous. No one is going to believe it. The story is a tangled mess. No one will ever believe it. So many competing narratives. Don't be foolish. It's preposterous that the government would take the words of some masturbating pothead writer no one has ever heard of and use those words in dozens of televisions shows to catch terrorists. My god even Pynchon couldn't dream of it.

—No one believes them anymore, except the fanatics and the cynics. The fanatics will follow them off the cliff and the cynics will follow the money. It's the end. It's the end of the world and nothing is as it seems.

—You're being dramatic Raymond.

—Do as you please. Guzman has the name. He has the story.

—That's all it is: a story.

—Yes, said Ray, standing up, that's all it is. But that proves my point not yours.

—They'll kill him, Raymond. Do you want that on your conscience? They'll accident him to death and I'll watch it on the news in a chalet in Switzerland or an apartment in Paris. You could join me.

—Probably, he said, but history has its own ideas. And no straight thing ever grew from a crooked timber.

—Spare me Raymond. Books are dead.

—Probably... *mais on ne se bat pas dans l'espoir du succès.*

—Oh for fuck's sake, Raymond. This is not one of your stories.

—Of course it is, he said, and he dropped a twenty on the table, took his coat and hat from the hook on the wall, put them on and walked out of the bar into the bright sunlight flooding the city.

ॐॐ

Senator Magic Bullet

Utta is on her knees under the senator's desk and sucking his cock while he speaks on the phone to another senator and when he shoots his load into her mouth he tightens his lips over his teeth and laughs in perfect rhythm to what's being said.

✿✿

The Engine of Intelligent Design

Winter's lurching, frost and shadows split in two, the force of attraction repels all understanding but one in many, the ache and furrows wound deep to spring fractured life into impossible bloom, always beast embracing saint.

✿✿

A Conversation Continued

—Tell me, said Guzman, did you intend to shoot her, or did you just miss the glass and hit her instead?

—I had returned from a journey. I had a knife. It meant something to me.

—What doesn't matter to a man?

—Is that a quote?

—It is now, said Guzman. But the knife?

—I purchased it in the Free Zone in Tegusa.

—And?

—A man came. It's a traditional thing, a custom. The man with the whetstone comes to sharpen your knives. You know he's coming because he plays a tune on his pipe. A reed pipe.

—Mythic, said Guzman, laughing, pipes of Pan and a knife.

—Like joining the world of missing persons.

—Is that a quote?

—It is now, said Ariel, it is now. But we are just talking heads I suppose.

—And the knife?

—I was overcome with a profound sadness as if the end of the road and every aborted soul arrived together in the moment of the knife, and on the blade I saw the words of everyone slipping out into the void.

—Dramatic, said Guzman.

Ariel paused and considered the window, the red rain drawing down the panes in lines and curves.

—Denial of the aborted is your problem, not mine. I am someone who burrows. I am a writer. I observe what it is like to wear the same suit to both a wedding and a funeral.

—I don't understand?

—Exactly.

—The shooting.

—I was aiming at myself.

—And shot Ms. Pepe in the head.

—A magic bullet has its own designs.

—It is not believable—

—What isn't?

—Facts.

—Facts are a matter of the utmost faith.

—Sophistry.

—The energy of delusion.

—You killed her.

—We killed her.

—We shall not hang for it.

—We shall all hang for it. Of that you may be certain.

✠ ✠

Tiresias Agonistes

"No amount of law enforcement can solve a problem that goes back to the family."

— J. Edgar Hoover

✠ ✠

The Fox

(A Story about Samantha and her Friends that Occurs Later in the Narrative)

She called her father Bulldaddy and they were from the south, the impoverished south, the south of fact and the south of fiction, of myth and movies and television; and her father was the kind of drunk who drank but showed no signs of the booze and was a small, quiet man married to a behemoth of a woman who talked and talked, and talked some more after that, and their daughter called him Bulldaddy and if you couldn't laugh at that and if you weren't scared to death by that, then you were a fool and life was going to step on you in one way or another and hard until you were broken but functional like a piece of old furniture sitting on a back porch with patches of rust and its seat sagging and the mesh hanging down like strands of something sad that no one had the energy to cut away or just get rid of, and you would become a fixture in the parade that started with whatever it was that made those two the kind that they were—him with the drinking and the whatever-pain of his diminutive stature and her with the stigma of her height and her size and his epic silences and the not-knowing of what it was he was doing (but knowing all the same) while his daughter called him Bulldaddy and came and went to parties you attended reluctantly because of obligations and affection for someone who had known her and said they had once been friends before she (of the bull and the daddy) had begun the impossible paradoxical climb up the social ladder in which the more she advanced, the more she fell as she wanted what she'd never have which was her father's approval and her mother's transformation and that was the story of all of that contained even in the faint knocking of melting ice cubes at the bottom of a glass of vodka she was drinking at a party where you all sat outside at a nice table on a beautiful early summer evening in the town that was the foyer of the empire across the river that was itself an open vein of history churning hard and still slow like blood seeping into everything as a reminder and a fetish of memory.

That was in a quiet place in the proper neighborhood in which one of that crew had found a home and it was a nice home with a long back lawn and a place under a tall tree for a table and the women were encased in drink and bitterness and wanting—wanting to climb and have power and status and the ability to flaunt their status only by saying, 'this is where I had dinner and this is where my friends spend their time,' and they turned their eyes on one another saying without words but only in gestures and looks, 'I will abandon you if it will get me ahead of you in this line,' and there was laughing and bottles of wine and there was a man who had been in the Carolinas and been called up to perform Guard Duty in the capital and he spoke of the scraping of the bottom of the barrel saying all the men now were in their forties and nothing with broken this and ungainly that and low minds and seeking just some money and the relatively easy duty of looking to radar screens that looked over the city, and they all raised their glasses to the troops but not the war which was as hollow a ritual gesture as any other, for you could just as easily have belched or dropped your pants and mooned the silky night sky for all the difference it would have made and they spoke on about money and property and sometimes out of a sense of what they perceived to be politeness, they asked you about your plans and your goals because it was the language they spoke best and they could understand goals and accomplishing goals and checking the days off their to-do lists so as to have a tool to beat down their anxiety about failure and death and the endless lists of all the things they believed must be done and shallow nights in beds without being pressed down hard by the weight of a lover or touched with any gentleness, which if they had it true and genuine would have scared them and woken in them every fear of betrayal, and instead they watched television shows where women of mysterious chemical composition proclaimed that they did not need anyone to feel whole and complete, but were happy with themselves alone and late that night alone, staring into the small front yard of your friend's small home, you felt the universe spinning, spinning faster and faster as a ball on a fingertip and then as was always likely, it wobbled off the point and fell bouncing to the ground, though that was just a metaphor and the yard secluded in the dark of the late late sacred night was just the yard, and from within the small wood near the rise of the freeway there came the strange yelping of the resident fox who moved as if he were his own tunnel burrowing in the dark and full of knowledge that only he would ever posses of how the earth beat as a heart and the drum of our time was sounding without let-up, but full of the terrible mercy of all true things.

THE END

San Francisco-Athens-Jerusalem-Alexandria-Baltimore

About the Author

Charles Talkoff is from New York and currently resides in Baltimore. His short stories and other works have appeared in such publications as *Underground Voices*, the *Urbanite*, the *Midway Journal*, *JMWW*, and *3 Quarters*. *The Love Song of J. Edgar Hoover* is his first novel.

Select 8th House Titles

CROSSING TO TADOUSSAC by Frederick E. Bryson

The FLQ have bombed the Montreal Stock Exchange. The streets are charged and a referendum is called on secession. Frederick E. Bryson captures a defining moment in Canadian history in his latest novel "Crossing to Tadoussac". 438 pages, 5 x 8, ISBN 978-1-926716-00-8

KOLKATA DREAMS by K. Gandhar Chakravarty

A work that will transport you across the sea to the idealization and mysticism of the East against the realities of its westernization. Reading and reciting this poetry, you will find that laughter often chokes itself on tears while the book yo-yos between meditation and contemplation. "*A robust, deceptive simplicity hums at the center of this collection...*" - YUSEF KOMUNYAKAA, PULITZER PRIZE WINNER FOR POETRY ON "KOLKATA DREAMS" Colour, Illustrated. ISBN 978-0-9809108-7-2

JUMP THE DEVIL by Richard Rathwell

With Jump the Devil, Richard Rathwell has masterfully interwoven the plots of five seemingly unrelated storylines to create one coherent narrative that spans the globe and works to blend the seemingly mundane with the profound, deftly providing readers the necessary clues to unlocking the story. Transcending borders, cultures, generations, and social mores, Jump the Devil brings to life the notion of the global village as it exists in the 21st Century. *Rathwell's writing is "a fistful of sentences written with the subtlety of a geisha and the terse certainty of stainless steel."* - JOHN OLSON, AUTHOR 5 X 8. 146 PAGES, ISBN 978-1-926716-11-4. $18.88

HYPODROME by Jason Price Everett

Jason Price Everett's poetry explodes from the page with the raucous power of industrial machinery and strikes its targets with the rapier's fine point. Honing in on the chaos of the past two decades, Hypodrome charts the growth of today's artist searching for the defining aesthetic of our time. These poems document the plastic, the losses, the frustrations and the triumphs accumulated during the course of an accelerated era set against the backdrop of an ominously beautiful future. 148 pages, 5 x 8 ISBN: 978-1-926716-12-1

UNFICTIONS by Jason Price Everett

Unfictions serves to dramatize the way in which we react to such an information-rich environment in all of its glorious simultaneity - the beginning of a type of 'New Realism' in letters - reflecting faithfully a society so saturated with events and quotations that it can no longer distinguish between them and their relative meanings. " "*...a remarkable achievement and issues a profound challenge to the literary landscape of today.*" - THE ANTIGONISH REVIEW ON "UNFICTIONS" 288 pages, 5 x 8. ISBN 978-0-9809108-6-5

THE MIDAS TOUCH BY James Cummins & Cameron W. Reed

"*... a journey into the predatory nature of some of the practices and institutions in the financial industry today ....*" Authors James Cummins and Cameron W. Reed take us on an exploratory journey into the predatory nature of some of the practices and institutions in the financial industry today. What seems innocently enough as capitalism and greed gone naturally wild in an environment of deregulation, soon appears as deliberate political manoeuvering and close control on an international scale by agents and institutions operating above the law. 230 pages. ISBN 978-1-926716-06-0 $23.88

Visit us online at www.8thHousePublishing.com